Benjamin Brierley

Spring Blossoms and Autumn Leaves

Benjamin Brierley

Spring Blossoms and Autumn Leaves

ISBN/EAN: 9783337366568

Printed in Europe, USA, Canada, Australia, Japan

Cover: Foto ©Andreas Hilbeck / pixelio.de

More available books at **www.hansebooks.com**

Spring Blossoms
AND Autumn Leaves

By Ben Brierley

Author of Tales & Sketches of Lancashire Life

Shackleton

"Whilst Dryads, decked in dewy gems," &c

MANCHESTER:
PUBLISHED BY J. ANDREW & Co., 1, WARREN STREET, OFF CROSS STREET

MANCHESTER :

J. ANDREW & CO., PRINTERS, 1, WARREN STREET, CROSS STREET.

1893.

INTRODUCTION.

BIOGRAPHICAL SKETCH

FROM *Momus*, 1879.

A GALLERY of Lancashire worthies would be indeed incomplete without the well-known features of Ben Brierley, whose name is a "household word" in every home, and whose individuality is a type of Lancashire pathos and humour with all its quaint conceits and dialectic mannerisms. He has achieved his popularity not only by voluminous literary work, but by a large-hearted and discreet philantrophy that endeavours to elevate the class from which he sprung by calling attention to its wants and grievances, and at the same time instilling those habits of self-help and self-control, without which all charitable organizations are simply worthless. Mr. Brierley was born at the Rocks, in Failsworth, June 26th, 1825. He attended the school in that village till his sixth year, when his parents, who were in very humble circumstances, removing to Hollinwood, little Benny lost the advantages of a day school, his services being required at the bobbin-wheel. But to him who is bent on self-improvement, difficulties are only obstacles to be surmounted, and at the Hollinwood Night and Primitive Methodist Sunday Schools, our hero was grafted in the rudiments of the three R's, and such was his love for reading, that at the very early age of seven, he had read his bible through no less than three times. In 1840 he returned to Failsworth Old School, and was

instrumental in forming a Mutual Improvement Society, which
proved to be the germ of a Mechanics' Institute. To an uncle,
who was a leading spirit in that school he owes his introduction
to Shakspere, Byron, and Shelley, the perusal of whose works
had a marked effect on his future career,

> " And lured him on to those inspiring toils
> By which man masters men."

At any rate, about this time his " muse began to labour," and one
of the very first deliveries was a sketch entitled " My uncle's
garden," commemorative of the Sunday mornings spent there in
happy and edifying conversation, which was, as Brierley says,
something to be remembered for a lifetime. This sketch was
published in 1849, in the supplement of the *Manchester Spectator* ;
but his labours, consecutively as hand-loom weaver, piecer, and
silk warper, prevented him for some time from following the bent
of his inclination. When we state that for nine years he had to
walk to and from his work nine miles each day our readers may
imagine he had but little time for the cultivation of his literary
faculties, and it was only during those peregrinations to and fro
that he could find time to indulge in reading, which had now
become one of the necessities of his existence. In 1855 he married ;
and, shortley afterwards, work in his branch of trade failing,
accepted the sub-editorship of the *Oldham Times*, but left that
situation in 1862, having obtained a short engagement in London.
During his stay in the metropolis he was introduced to the Savage
Club, and made the acquaintance of the Brough Brothers, Andrew
Halliday, Tom Robertson, and other well-known dramatic
celebrities. When *Colman's Magazine* which had been started by
members of the club, collasped, Mr. Brierley returned to Manchester, where he has since resided, settling down as an author
and reader of his own works, in both of which capacities he has
achieved a popularity second to no man in the county. The
library of a Lancashire home would indeed be incomplete without
the works of Ben Brierley—his unadulterated patois being alike
relished by his readers and hearers throughout the whole
Palatinate.

Mr. Brierley's married and literary career may be said to be co-existent, for in 1855 was written " Jimmie the Jobber " a little story which he submitted to a friend, who strongly advised him not to publish it ; but, stimulated by the success of Edwin Waugh, whose "Come whoam to thi childer an' me " had about that time rendered its author famous, he resolved to publish it in one form or another, and the sketch appeared in the *Manchester Spectator*, and, being afterwards published in book form, had a good sale, as had also his succeeding ventures. His success led to his introduction to the editor of the *Weekly Times*, and he at once commenced to write for the supplement of that journal. But strong as was Brierley's attachment to journalistic literature, his love of the drama was still stronger; and, aspiring to histrionic honours, he produced a dramatic version of his " Layrock of Langleyside," in which he himself played the principal part, and achieved a decided success as an impersonator of Lancashire character. As an author, Mr. Brierley possesses the qualifications of genial humour and touching pathos ; and his early associations have given him a grip of his subject of which he has not been slow to avail himself, his mind being quick to appropriate those quaint oddities of Lancashire life which his keen eye is ever ready to detect.

A turning point in his life was the institution of *Ben Brierley's Journal*, which attained great popularity, and a marvellous circulation, the " gude fowk " of Lancashire being delighted with the bright and healthy stories, written in their own idiomatic language, and with a grasp of their social characteristics which an intimate acquaintance can alone evolve. Though Ben's poetry is overshadowed by his prose, he has an undeniable poetic temperament, and some of his shorter pieces are real gems. In a short sketch like this we cannot enumerate his multitudinous works which, if we mistake not, have been published in a complete form in some fifteen or twenty volumes.

In the November of 1875 Mr. Brierley was elected a City Councillor, and although his candidature had been almost regarded as a joke, Ab'-o'th'-Yate was not long in proving to his constituents that their confidence had not been misplaced. His maiden speech was in support of the Free Libraries Committee's successful attempt to prevent the Reference Department being located in the attic of the New Town Hall. The peroration will be long remembered by the parody on Longfellow's " Excelsior," the concluding lines of which were as follow—

> "Oh! what would Grundy say, or Lamb,
> If, without aid of 'bus or tram.
> They sought up there their heads to cram :
> All right Excelsior—but d—n
>   The Town Hall Stairs."

On resuming his seat, amid shouts of laughter and applause, Alderman Lamb rose to reply, but confessed it required considerable nerve to follow the new councillor. Ben Brierley had made his mark, and the first vacancy found him one of the Free Libraries Committee. His municipal experiences, more especially in connection with the Nuisances Committee, led him to raise the question " What shall we do with our poor ?" No man was better qualified to give an opinion on the subject, and the dailies, by ventilating the question, proved that he had hit the right nail on the head. The Artisans' Dwelling Act, although shelved by the Health Committee, was another instance of Brierley's sympathies for the humbler classes ; and his letter on the " Domestic Economy Congress," entitled *A Flourish of Trumpets* was described by a well-known barrister as a " skinner."

His sphere of usefulness may be most aptly described by the fact that he has, during his municipal career, served on a greater number of Committees and Sub-Committees of General purposes, than perhaps any other member of the Corporation, viz : " Nuisances," " Hackney Coach," " Lamp and Scavenging," " Free Libraries," " Parks and Cemeteries," and " Baths and Wash-houses Committees," " Public Rooms and Printing and Stationery Sub-Committees."

Here is an amount of work of which any Councillor may well be proud ; but in addition to this Mr. Brierley, in connection with the relief organisations during the past winter, assisted on the platform in no less than twenty-two entertainments, his services always being gratuitous, even to the payment of his personal expenses.

Such a man may well be popular, and when Ab'-o'th'-Yate crosses the Atlantic, on a visit to our American cousins, during the ensuing autumn, and such I believe is his intention, thousands of admirers will not only wish him God speed, but a quick return to the old country—spots which his graphic pen has rendered dear to many a town-dweller. I have before alluded to his dramatic instincts, and may as well call attention to the fact that he, in conjunction with his friend Mr. Dottie, will appear during the month of September at the Theatre Royal, in his own drama of "The Lancashire Weaver Lad." The occasion will be a most interesting one, and no doubt advantage will be taken of such an opportunity to prove to Ben Brierley the estimation in which he is held by his fellow-citizens.

INDEX.

TO ALL GOOD AND TRUE

FREEMASONS,

FROM

HIS ROYAL HIGHNESS THE PRINCE OF WALES

DOWNWARDS,

THIS BOOK IS, WITH BROTHERLY

AFFECTION, INSCRIBED.

HARPURHEY,
    MANCHESTER.

MAY.

(*Manchester Guardian*, 1854.)

MAY is come!—the month of flowers,—
　　O'er the banks, and through the bowers,
Laughing breezes, light and gay,
Bear the greeting—" Welcome May!"
　Drinking ether as he sings,
Flashing sunlight from his wings,
The soaring lark, with merry throat,
Warbles shrill his Maying note.
Other songsters from the grove,
Pour their matin songs of love,
And blithely hop from spray to spray,
Hailing nature's holiday.
　Trooping down the vale below,—
Weaving garlands as they go;
Sweet as heav'nly seraphim,
Little vale nymphs chant their hymn,—
　" Come, ye children, hither come,
Through the woodlands let us roam,
And chase the wand'ring butterfly,
Ere he seeks some other sky.
Let us go where flowery banks
Offer up their morning thanks,
To the home of every pray'r,

For the pretty robes they wear.
There watch how fairy hands distil
Sparkling wine-drops from the rill;
And pass the cup from flow'r to flow'r,
To celebrate the festal hour;
Whilst Dryads,* decked in dewy gems.
  Gaily trip it o'er the lea,
To tiny bells, on nodding stems,
  Ringing elfin minstrelsy.
Merry shouts ring through the dell;
Ling'ring whispers haunt the well;
Echo calls from far away,
List ye what its voices say—
  " Away, and seek the greenwood shade
Come each village youth and maid,
Bring ye flowers fresh and gay,
To strew before the Queen of May.
Here are dainties to allure
From his feast the epicure;
For the simple honey bee
Hath a sweeter feast than he.
Bring the old, the hale, the young,—
Bring the feeble and the strong,
To watch the merry pranking troop
Round the flow'ry May Queen group.
Mingle in the dance and song,
All who would their lives prolong,
And ne'er rest till shadows gray
Indicate the close of day,
For 'tis May! 'tis May! 'tis May!

* Dryads, wood nymphs.

WIGAN SAM.

THERE is in Bury's ancient town
    An inn of good report ;
'Tis not the "Albion," " Keys," nor "Queens,"
    Nor one of humbler sort.

But high it towers above the roofs
    Of " Swans," "Grey Mares," and "Grapes ;"
And many a peddling hostelry,
    Its grander neighbour apes.

But none can match the " Eagle's Nest "
    In quality of fare,
Though some aver the figure's high ;
    But such are poor and rare.

The cream of good society,
    The privileged, and proud,
Have on our inn, for years gone by,
    Their patronage bestowed.

Look on the stately front, and say
    Who of plebeian soil
Shall e'er presume to take it's wines,
    Or share the barmaid's smile ?

The host, than whom a neater man
    Is known in Bury town,
Can either welcome with a bow,
    Or freeze you with a frown.

That means, when you're good company,
    Or tavern laws transgress ;
But though he turns on points so nice,
    Esteem him not the less.

A wit he is, and fond of joke,
    Albeit of high degree ;
And though he courts a coronet,
    To lowly worth is free.

What can be said of man the more,
    However high his birth ?
The wight who owns a generous heart
    Is emperor of the earth !

A tyke there came to Bury town,
    One " Wigan Sam " by name ;
A dog whom neither house, nor clan,
    Nor parish cared to claim.

Friends he had none, nor kith, nor kin,—
    No home wherein to creep
When winds were fierce, and frosts were keen,
    And snows were wild and deep,

Save the " big house " upon the hill,
    Where dwell the lost to earth—
Where feeds the vagabond beside
    The wreck of humble worth.

Sam lay in fallow half his time
    Within those sheltering walls,

Nor sought to lift by fruitful toil
   Himself to higher calls.

But when the flowers began to peep,
   And birds began to sing,
And nettles grew on sunny banks—
   The firstlings of the spring,—

Then Sam would from his furrow creep,
   And shaking off the earth
That pauper sloth had heaped on him,
   For change would wander forth.

'Mongst brick-crofts, farms, and buildings new,
   A living, Sam would make,
And sleep at nights in barn or stall,
   Or taproom lodgings take.

When other work could not be found,
   A basket he would sling,
And vend young onions, mustard, cress—
   The edibles of spring ;

Or he would trundle through the street,
   A one-wheeled truck, with sand
And " idle-back " for rags and bones,
   Or " aught " that came to hand.

But Sam had one ambitious wish,
   Though paltry it might seem,
To raise a modest donkey cart,
   With single brute, or team.

Yet how the needful to obtain,
  Such " rolling stock " to buy,
Had bothered oft his scheming pate,
  And turned his wits awry.

But, lucky thought ! each dog's his hour,
  And Sam's had come at last ;
His wand'rings through the streets one day
  The " Eyrie " led him past.

Mine host just out of band-box turned,
  Stood whistling at the door,
With hands deep in his pockets thrust,
  Their contents jingling o'er.

Our vagabond from Wigan town
  Soon Boniface espied,
And, waxing keen to try a joke,
  Thus to the yokel cried.

" Hollo, old sinner ! what's your game ?
  You're *out* again, I see.
No work ? Eh, eh ! Old story, Sam :
  Oh,—want to speak to me ?

Well, cut it short. What is't you want ?"
  "A friend," was Sam's reply ;
" I want to raise a suvverin
  A jackass cart to buy.

I know wheere I con have a moke
  Two days a week or so ;

An' if yo'n lend me th' twenty bob
    Yo'n be th' best friend I know."

" But what *security* can t' give ?"
    Mine host said with a grin ;
" A man these times must have some hold
    Before he parts with tin."

" That's bothered me for weeks an' months,"
    Said Sam with hopeful leer ;
" But now I've getten o'er it straight
    An' tidy. It's just here—

I're thinkin', if yo' lent me th' brass,
    Ut I could make a start,
For security, an' sich as that,
    Yo' could have yo'r name on th' cart."

OWD PIGEON.

"THE RULING PASSION STRONG IN DEATH."

OWD PIGEON wur as dry a brid
    As ever swiped his drink ;
He liked to see a frothy pint
    Smile at his nose, an' wink.

At morn or neet, 'twur aulus reet,
    A quart, or pint, or gill
Wur th' same to him ; if th' pot wur full
    He never had his fill.

If e'er he geet his breeches' knees
    Beneath a taproom table,
He'd sit, an' drink, an' smoke, an' wink
    As long as he wur able.

He'd grown so firm to th' alehouse nook,
    An' swiped so mony mixtures,
That when it coom to changin' honds
    He're reckoned among th' fixtures.

Whene'er their Betty brewed a " peck,"
    If he could find a jug,
He wouldno' wait till th' ale wur "tunned,"
    He'd lade it eaut o'th' mug.

One neet Owd Pigeon flew to'ard whoam,
    Wi' a very wobblin' flutter ;

Sometimes he'd tumble into th' hedge,
　　An' sometimes into th' gutter.

He knew he're late, an' didno' want
　　Their Betty t' see a leet ;
So crept upstairs to bed i'th' dark
　　An' in his stockin' feet.

He groped abeaut i'th' sleepin' cote,
　　An' felt for th' drawers an' th' bed ;
But nowt he touched till th' bedpost flew,
　　An' banged again his yead.

" Theigher," said Pigeon, " that's a go ;
　　There' someb'dy bin workin' charms ;
For it's th' fust time e'er I knew mi nose
　　Wur longer than mi arms."

But poor Owd Pigeon's time had come,
　　An' when his will he'd signt,
He said he ailed nowt nobbut " drooth,"
　　An' begged for another pint.

His " rulin passion " stuck till death,
　　An' as th' Slayer raised his dart,
He licked his lips, an' faintly said,
　　" Just mak' it int' a quart.

I wouldno' care a pin for th' grave,
　　Though I'm totterin' upo' th' brink,
If I could come back wi' th' buryin' folk,
　　An' ha' my share o'th' drink."

TO HER ROYAL HIGHNESS
THE DUCHESS OF EDINBURGH
ON HER WEDDING.

HAIL to thee, chick o'th' eagle hee,
    Ut flaps its wings o'er th' Baltic Sea ;
Theau'rt welcome to eaur Sal an' me,
        An' Walmsley Fowt.

Theau comes wi' th' snowdrops, fair as they,
Peepin' eaut at th' wintry day ;
But soon theau'll see an English May
        I' Lunnon Fowt.

Theau should ha' come'n some years bygone,
Just when I're shepst'rin'* th' owdest son,
Before thoose feights wur lost and won
        I'th' Crimean Fowt.

Theau met ha' saved us summat then,
I' peawther, gowd, an' lives o' men ;
But theau'd hardly crept fro' under th' hen,
        When th' War-cocks fowght.

Come o'er t'eaur heause—bring Alfred, too ;
Beaut him th' owd rib mit jealous groo—
We'n have a glorious Lanky brew,
        I' Walmsley Fowt.

* Shepst'rin, nursing.

We'n have a crimbly-crusted pie
O' Paddy's grapes; an' if theau'll try
A plateful on't, soon th' news 'll fly
        To Peter's fowt.

They'd raise a steeam o' Neva's shore
Would keep th' owd brook fro' freezin' o'er,
An' warm folk as they'rn ne'er warmed before,
        Not e'en wi' th' *Knout.*

I'll show thee what theau's seldom seen—
Some happier folks than king or queen;
Wheere warmer hearts an' breeter e'en
        Ne'er blessed a fowt.

For o that, we'r no' donned like thee,
I' silk an' gowd and fiddle-de-de:
Blue print is eaur best finery,
        I' Walmsley Fowt.

We are no' fed o' nilles rare;
An' yet we'n just a little t' spare
For folk ut han their cubborts bare,
        I' any fowt.

Theau's not had porritch twice a day,
As I've had mony a time, nor tae
Ut's tasted like a brew o hay,
        An' sometimes *nowt.*

It's hardly likely theau'll e'er see
A whitenin' lip an' glazin' e'e,
Through want o' that God sent for me,
          An' o i'th fowt.

Theau winno' yer a little moan
I'th neet-time, when theau'rt feelin' lone.
When lips han muttered—" Is there noane—
          No *bread* i'th' fowt ?"

But why wi' back-thowts fill my e'en ?
That th' wo'ld's groon breeter may be seen—
On every face, an' hearth, an' green,
          I' mony a fowt.

Theau's made it breeter wi' that star
O' promise theau's browt from afar,
Ut tells us love shall conquer war,
          I' every fowt.

Better' ha weddin'-bells than th' clang
O' glitterin' steel, or cannon's bang :
A welcomer peal than thine ne'er rang
          O'er ne'er a fowt.

Yo'r Alfred's thine an' England's pride—
Spotless he laft his mother's side ;
An' may no good that tongue betide
          Ut says he's prowt,

Look to him, then, wi' wifely care,
To keep him shy o' wicked snare ;
Guard him wi' booath hont an' prayer,
            When caut i'th' fowt ;

For princes are no common folk,
But marks at which to fire a joke,
An' dirty wits their fun to poke,
            I' every fowt.

That brother-in-law o' thine—yo'r Ned—
Ever sin' he their Alick wed,
Has had a deeal abeaut him said
            I' mony a fowt.

But I ne'er tak' o in ut's towd :
A mon may be as good as gowd,
An' scandil's tongue shall have him jowed
            An' pown to nowt.

If e'er th' owd woman meddles o' thee—
But surely that con never be—
Dunno' like some wives, goo on th' spree,
            An' tell o th' fowt ;

But use her kindly—hers has been
A life ne'er lived by other queen.
No wrong words ever passed between
            Her an' her fowt·

Walk theau i'th' track her shoon han made,
An' tak no heed o' whisperin' jade,
Ut yers things that han ne'er been said,
   I' ne'er a fowt.

Happen theau'll have a family—
A big un, sometime—we shall see.
If th' fust's a *lad*, then send for me
   To Walmsley Fowt ;

An' I'll be godfeyther to th' bab—
(Just tak' a hint an' co' him AB)—
Then wouldno' there be a a roarin' gab
   I' England Fowt ?

"OWD AB'S" LAMENT OVER KNOTT MILL FAIR.

AIR.—*The harp that once through Tara's Halls.*

THE lungs that once through Knott Mill Fair
    Their classic music shed,
Are now as mute in Knott Mill Fair
    As if that voice were dead.
So gone's the strut of former days,
    So tinselled glory's o'er ;
And hearts that beat to penny praise
    Now feel that throb no more.

No more the chief with tawdry dight
    The roar of tumult swells ;
The noise alone that's heard at night
    Its tale of drinkin' tells.
Thus talent now whene'er it wakes,
    Our feelings to engage,
Is when some poor old Thespian takes
    A taproom for a stage.

FOTCHIN TH' KEAWS UP.

O NE summer e'enin
        When the screenin
Cleauds drew o'er the settin sun.
        Madge went trippin
        Eaut o'th' shipp'n,—
Fotchin th' keaws, as oft hoo'd done.
        In th' owd lane
        Hoo met a swain
Pluckin blossoms from the spray.
        " Madge," said he,—
        " It's strange to see
Thee fotchin th' keaws so late i'th' day."

        Madge said nowt,
        Yet truly thowt
Ther summat wicked in his e'e :
        But when her waist
        He tightly pressed
Heaw could hoo longer silent be ?
        Hoo said—" Jim Dawson,
        Eh, theau fause un,
What dos't think my mam'll say,
        If hoo sees thee
        Offer t' squeeze me—
Fotchin th' keaws up late i'th' day ?

" Let me goo, Jim ;
Neaw, then, do, Jim—
Aw've no time for stoppin here."
But the youth,
To tell the truth,
Wi' cobweb could ha' held her theere :
Then the gate
Was not too strait
For two to pass, an' goo ther way :
But who could pass
A bonny lass,
When fotchin th' keaws up late i'th' day ?

" Madge," said Jim—
Whilst hoo to him
As closely clung as he to her—
" It's strange if time
I' th' summer's prime
An heaur to lovers conno spare.
If th' owd sun's gone,
Ther's th' young moon yon,
Stringin' silver beads on th' hay ;
An' thoos bits o'
Leet that flit so,
Are keaws hoo's fotchin' late i'th' day.

" Two cleauds meeting',
Neaw are greetin' ;
See 'em kissin' as they pass ?"
Madge, not thinkin'
Ill, said, shrinkin',
" Which is th' lad, an' which is th' lass ?"

" That," said Jim,
" Ut's breet an' slim,
Must be the lass, neaw on her way
Spreadin' charms
O'er heaven's farms,
Whilst fotchin th' keaws up late i'th' day."

'T had been a wonder
An' a blunder,
Had the skies their lessons lost ;
If two cleauds, meetin',
Did o'th' greetin',
Why did Jim the maid accost ?
But oh ! the kisses,
And the blisses,
That took Madge's heart away !
Neaw hoo's fain
Hoo met a swain
When fotchin th' keaws up late i'th' day.

THE BONNIE LAD WI' TH' APRON ON.*

(MASONIC SONG.)

*Music by Bro. Past Master N. Dumville. Manchester :
Hime and Addison ; Forsyth Brothers.*

MY JAMIE is a Mason bold
   His *mother's age* ten seventy seven
His word to me's as good as gold
   His soul's as pure as smile from Heaven.
Whene'er we take our walks at eve,
   A face for him—there's only one ;
Than lose his heart a world I'd give—
   My bonnie lad wi' th' apron on !

He jewels wears upon his breast,
   And three upon his brat so white ;
And when he's donned up in his best,
   Oh, is he not my heart's delight ?
He says I ought to cautious be
   When other lads try on their fun ;
But surely he's no doubts of me—
   My bonnie lad wi' th' apron on !

Why need he says he's on the square,
   And true his life to rule and plumb?
You'll find few young men anywhere,
   That virtues such as his become.

He kissed me at the gate to-neet,
  And now he to his lodge is gone ;
But later on I'm bound to meet
  My bonnie lad wi' th' apron on.

A day he's named—a day to come,
  When I must take the first degree
In the Free Masonry of home,
  Then happy sister shall I be.
His secrets I already know,
  And in the grips we both are one ;
A spotless vesture soon I'll show
  My bonnie lad wi' th' apron on !

*Dedicated to Bro. Colonel Le Gendre N. Starkie, Rt. Worshipful Prov. Grand Master of Masons in East Lancashire.

FALL OF SEBASTOPOL.

HUSH! methought I heard a sound,
　　As 'twere a booming thunder-burst,
Awake the startled echoes 'round,
　　And cleave the midnight air.　The first
Hath scarcely died ere pealing flies
A second volley to the skies:—
A third! and now a crash of bells
The new-born tale of triumph tells.

　　Strange whispers pass from door to door,
Which grow to shouts from street to street,
　　'Till swelling in one distant roar,—
Where rushing myriads, myriads meet,
Is climax'd by one thundering voice—
　　　　　" Sebastopol hath fallen!"

　　　　　　　　Rejoice,
Ye youths and maidens of the land;
Ye grey-haired sires, a noble band;
Ye mothers of a race as brave
As ever fought on field, or wave,—
Rejoice! this is no time to mourn,
Though heroes bleed and cities burn.
From crimson rain shall vineyards flow,—
From smouldering ashes harvests grow.

　　Beside a humble cottage door
A woman stood, who oft before
Had lingered there to read of wars,
As presaged in the book of stars.

At times the face of heaven would seem
As if illumed by glory's beam.
At others, drops of lurid light
Would leave the sky to blackest night.
Then would despair the watcher seize,
Who, falling on her suppliant knees,
Would pray—and would 'twere not in vain!—
Her " Geordie" might come home again.

    " What does it mean ?" the woman cries,
As past her door a neighbour flies.
" What does it mean ?—What does it mean ?
The war is o'er,—God bless the Queen !"
" The war is o'er ; and England won !
Then shall I see—again—my son."
Yes, in thy visions, woman grey,
But not in dance or revel gay.
Look, where the battle's smoke divides ;
Where 'mongst the slain the victor rides ;
There see, the rising cloud reveals
A form that from a saddle reels.
A wound, made by a sabre stroke,
Like winter sun through fog and smoke,
Or iron bar in heated forge,
Marks for the grave thy darling George.

    " What will they say in England now ?"
Exclaims the youth, with bleeding brow.
" Alas ! I shall not hear what's said,
For now I'm quartered with the dead !"
Then takes he from his breast a charm,
Worn not to shield from battle's harm,

But one to kiss at evening prayer—
It is a lock of silver hair.

　　" What will they say in mine own land ?"
Exclaims a youth of another band.
Victorious you, and conquered we—
Though why we fought's unknown to me.
That fatal cut was from my sword,
And your own steel my blood hath gored !"
Then takes he from his breast a charm,
Worn not to shield from battle's harm,
But one to kiss at evening prayer—
It is a lock of golden hair.

　　Two hands are clasped in death's embrace :
Two foes are prostrate, face to face.
" You leave a mother," said the one—
His power of utterance nearly gone :
" I leave a wife and children dear ;
And 'twas not glory led me here.
They said 'twas fealty to the Czar
That forced his subjects into war.
But why it was that I slew you,
Or why it was that me you slew,
Is not for us but kings to say,
On Greater Field and Greater Day."

　　Locked in each other's arms, the twain
Were told at roll-call with the slain.
As foes they fought, as friends they bled—
The martyr triumph of the dead.
What holier voice could sound afar
A protest 'gainst the sin of war ?

THE WAVERLOW BELLS.

OLD Jammie and Ailse went a-down the brookside,
Arm-in-arm, as when young, before Ailse was a
bride;
And what made them pause near the Hollybank wells?
'Twas to list to the chimes of the Waverlow bells.

"How sweet," said old Jammie, "How sweet on the ear,
Comes the ding-donging sound of yon curfew, my dear!"
But old Ailse ne'er replies—for her bosom now swells—
Oh, she loved in her childhood those Waverlow bells.

"Thou remember'st," said Jammie "the night we first
met,
Near the Abbey Field gate—the old gate is there yet—
When we roamed in the moonlight, o'er fields and
through dells,
And our hearts beat along with the Waverlow bells.

" And then that wakes morning, so early at church,
When I led thee a bride through the old ivy porch,
And our new home we made where the curate now dwells,
And we danced to the music of Waverlow bells.

"And when that wakes morning came round the next
year,
How we bore a sweet child to the christ'ning font there;
But our joy-peals soon changed to the saddest of knells,
And we mourned at the sound of the Waverlow bells."

Then in silence, a moment, the old couple stood,
Their hearts in the churchyard, their eyes on the flood :
And the tear, as it starts, a sad memory tells—
Oh ! they heard a loved voice in those Waverlow bells.

" Our Ann," said old Ailse, " was the fairest of girls ;
She had heaven in her face, and the sun in her curls;
Now she sleeps in a bed where the worm makes its cells,
And her lullaby's sung by the Waverlow bells."

" But her soul," Jammie said, " she'd a soul in her eyes,
And their brightness is gone to its home in the skies :
We may meet her there yet, where the good spirit dwells,
When we'll hear them no more—those old Waverlow
        bells."

Once again—only once— this old couple were seen
Stepping out in the gloaming across the old green,
And to wander adown by the Hollybank wells,
Just to list to the chimes of the Waverlow bells.

Now the good folks are sleeping beneath the cold sod,
But their souls are in bliss with their daughter and God,
And each maid in the village now mournfully tells
How old Jammie and Ailse loved the Waverlow bells.

THE BONNIE BLUE RIBBON.

'TWAS down in the vale,
  Where the Medlock runs clear,
That I met with young Colin,
  In the fall of the year.
The glance that he gave,
  Made my heart bound with glee,—
He'd a bonnie blue ribbon,
  Tied under his knee.

He asked for my heart,
  But he'd had it before ;
If I'd twenty to give,
  I'd have given him a score.
My looks must have told him
  What I could not see,—
Oh, the bonnie blue ribbon,
  Tied under the knee.

His voice is so tender,
  So mellow and sweet,
Which the thrush in the gloaming
  Its tones would repeat.
The mirth of the village
  No charm had for me ;
'Twas the bonnie blue ribbon,
  Tied under the knee.

But woe's me, my love
  Has been pressed to the wars;
He'll return crowned with glory,
  Or covered with scars.
If the fates be as kind,
  As his heart's been to me,
He'll wear the blue ribbon,
  Tied under the knee.

The summer is past
  And the birds are all fled,
Yet no word of my Colin,
  Is he living, or dead?
If he'd send me a line,
  'Twould be hearts-ease to me:
Or the bonnie blue ribbon,
  Tied under the knee.

Oh, why this strange feeling.
  This hope and this fear?
There's something that tells me
  My lover is near.
'Tis my Colin come back,
  To his home, and to me:
With the bonnie blue ribbon.
  Tied under his knee.

TO MY WIFE.

NOW " all that glitters is not gold,"
    A lesson learn from that, dear wife !
The sun that's bright at morning-tide,
    Is like the transient morn of life.
At noon it pales its morning beams ;
    The sky assumes a sober grey,
As if the calm of eventide,
    Would chase in sleep all cares away.

Another morn, a brighter morn,
    May greet with joy our waking hour,
A sun of Heavenly gold may shine,
    Not plated o'er by earthly power,
But gemmed as with a coronal,
    Formed of the purest crystal ray,
And stream afar, like an angel's smile ;
    The light of an Eternal day.

HALL STREET, MOSTON,
    April 29th, 1893.

WELCOME TO OUR OLD FRIEND,
"BEN."

WELCOME, "Owd Brid!" We give thee hearty
     cheer,
  In this, the happiest place of all thy life.
Oft have we heard thee sing, with voice so clear,
  Of all the charms with which it is so rife.

Here hast thou gazed, as only Poets can,
And felt the landscape not the work of man ;
And, gazing thus, thy soul has filled with light,
To brighten up the wearied "Cotter's Night ;"
And, bursting forth in many a joyous strain,
Hast made the welkin fairly ring again.

And now that thou dost come to bid " Adieu !"
  To all the scenes that made thy boyhood bright,
And hast the Valleys of the West in view
  (Yet none so happy as *this one* to-night),
We bid thee welcome ; and, with hearts made light,
Would cheer up thine, that it may now feel right.

Come ! keep thi drooping "pecker" up, "owd lad,"
It will no' do that *thou* shouldst now be sad ;
We'll keep thy memory dear—and fresh and green—
Though other features come upon the scene.

We'll not forget " Owd Ab," nor all his ways ;
   And when he's landed on yon distant shore,
May riches crown the warbling of his lays,
   And all his sighings and his cares be o'er.

May " mighty dollars" rain upon his path,
   And comforts give (which here have been but few),
That what he there may get, and what he hath,
   Be quite sufficient for the end in view.

And should he, as the dreary months roll on,
   For England and for Failsworth once more pine,
We'll hail the ship that brings us back a Son,
   And give him welcome with a loud " lang syne ;"
We'll sing " lang syne" with *all* our might and main,
And welcome back our OLD FRIEND BEN again.

                      JULIUS.

March 28th, 1884.

TO BENJAMIN BRIERLEY, ESQ.,

In View of his Leaving this Country for a Tour
in the U. S. A.

(Copyright.)

FAREWELL! thou son of song :
　　Well dost thou stand among
Th' *elite* of men !
Thy name and fame are great :
We now congratulate
In full and fitting state,
　　Thy gifted pen.

Thy pen has facile pow'r !
In volumetric show'r
　　And gifted grace ;
Thy quill has writ of truth
And beauty : and, forsooth,
Of man : his moral growth
　　And chequered race.

c

Perchance in yon great land-
The deep blue sea beyond—
    A welcome sweet ;
Replete with gen'rous love,
And sweet as voice of dove,
In tidal waves may move
    Thy soul to greet.

The people there are great
In virtue and in state—
    A noble race !
Their speech is England's tongue ;
Their life is grand and young ;
Their love is pure and strong :
    Go thou and trace.

A joyous voyage then,
To thee, beloved " Ben,"
    And safe return !
O'er ocean's rudest wave
May He, that's mighty, save
A life that's more than brave :
    Then we'll not mourn.

                                    ARNICA.

Moston Priory, Manchester,
    March 5th, 1884.

LANCASHIRE'S BEN.

EACH branch of Art and Science boasts,
Within our own and other coasts,
Peculiarly its famous Ben,
Who sways by tongue or brush or pen.
The world of politics, you'll own,
Few bolder than Ben Dizzy's known.
The Drama —ne'er to be effaced—
By "rare Ben Jonson" has been graced,
And by Ben Webster, eke, I ween—
Illumined by their talents' sheen!
Ben Franklin, philosophic guide!
Achieved renown as fair as wide;
While as a painter, lo, Ben West,
By Western States is counted *best*.
Nay, nature, high o'er woods and glens,
Displays and revels in her Bens:
Ben Nevis, and Ben Lomond, too;
Ben Ledi and brave Ben Venue.
E'en London has its own " Big Ben,"
O'er its Cathedral reared by Wren.

And in this busy shire, we ken
A glorious and victorious Ben,
With greenest laurels on his brow,
Whom it delights to honour now,
With golden tokens of regard,
As author, humorist, and bard––
Oh, say, where shall we meet a life
With truer love of freedom rife.
More free from spurious sentiments,
More in the people's welfare spent ?
His banter, when in fullest play,
Is sparkling as the summer's ray ;
His wit, though keen as rapier found,
Unlike the rapier, ne'er doth wound :
His homely virtues him endear
To hosts of friends both far and near,
Who bid him " God-speed " o'er the main,
And wish him safely home again !

JAMES HOLDEN.

Rochdale.

FAREWELL TO AMERICA.

FAREWELL, land of "booms," "tickets,"
    "platforms," and "vetoes,"
Of lightening bugs, whistling frogs, snakes and
    mosquitoes,
Land of fried oysters, of clam-bakes, and chowder,
And the rowdy's best arguments, bullets and powder;
Land of all races, all colours, and mixings,
Of candy and peanuts, of notions and fixings,
Where prohibitive laws do not stop folks from drinking,
But old Bourbon and rye can be had for the winking.
Where a man who robs banks is held up as a "smart
    one;"
But let him take bread that will just keep life's cart on,
He'll get it quite hot from the judge who ne'er justice
    meant,
And sent up for weeks to the home of the penitent.
Land of "road agents," of pedlars, and "drummers,"
Of confidence tricksters, "bushwhackers," and
    "bummers,"
Where political knaves fatten out of the taxes,
And how they get hold of them no man e'er "axes."

If I tell thee thy faults 'tis because that I love thee,—
Oh, land of the free ! while the bird soars above thee,
That swoops on thy foes like thy blizzards and cyclones,
'Twixt thee and old England may bygones be bygones !
Do what has been done by thy mother before thee,
Deeds blazoned in history, ballad, and story ;
Drive out the vile rascals that plunder thy coffers,
And cease to be jeered at by railers and scoffers.
Take the bull by the horns,—not the " John " of that
    " aire " name ;
And throw down the beast that has trod on thy fair
    fame ;
'Twill have to be done either sooner or later,--
So here's to the doing of 't my " darlin' young crater ! "
' So long ! "*

*So Long. The American term for " good bye ! "

A "DAUGHTER OF EVE."

A BLACKPOOL IDYL.

PENSIVE she sat—alone—upon the pier,
　　Watching the setting sun its lessening disc
Dip in the western wave.　And long she gazed.
Andromeda, held captive in the sea,
Was not more sad than she—sad beyond tears.
I picture to myself the fading form
Of some fair barque, bound for a foreign shore,
And with it all she loved on earth.
I tried to read her thoughts.　Were maidens fair,
And matchless in their beauty, in that land
Towards where the swelling sails their canvas bent?
And would a glance from their dark eyes so fill
The soul with the sweet ecstasy of love,
That *he'd* forget the love he'd left behind?
She'd heard of syrens hid in ocean caves
That so beguile the faithless mariner
With soul-enslaving harmonies, that he
Forgets he's mortal, and's for ever lost.
Anon she did avert her face, then cast
Her eyes again across the angry deep.
I ventured to ask the cause of all her grief—
Why she, like Niobe, was all in tears?
She sighed, and said—" *Wait till I get him whoam !*"

BURNS'S BIRTHDAY.

POETICAL ADDRESS, DELIVERED AT AN IMAGINARY FESTIVAL.

O YE wha hae nae higher aims
    Than fill wi' drink your drouthy wames,
Ye need hae schoolings frae your dames
                When ye forget
That nichts are langer at your hames
                Than where ye set.

I am nae Solomon, nor sage,
Whose virtue only comes with age,
Who war eternal nightly wage
                'Gainst saups o' drink ;
But tak a drop i' " Tammy's Cage "
                To mak 'em wink.

This day young Rab first saw the light
Shine o'er his head—a wond'rous sight !
'Twas like a holy nimbus, bright,
                To greet his birth.
Then darkness skelpit like the night
                Frae off the earth.

He saw around him as he grew,
A grabbin, keen, and selfish crew,
To naething but their int'rests true
　　　　　　　The God they serve.
Aught good in man they naething knew
　　　　　　　To make them swerve.

On hypocrite he laid the stick
They kept for decent folk, an' sic
As woulda, like dumb spaniels, lick
　　　　　　　Their dirty neive.
(I maun keep friendly wi' Auld Nick,
　　　　　　　He hauds my brief.)

He made the sanctimonious squeal,
Like rattons in an empty biel ;
The Sunday saint an' Monday de'il
　　　　　　　He wouldna spare :
But like a doughty, honest chiel,
　　　　　　　He'd strip them bare.

But in his gentler nature he
In wounded hare a friend could see ;
Or birdie, wounded wantonly.
　　　　　　　(They ca' it game
A bairn sae scared, an' canno flee,
　　　　　　　Is just the same).

For poor auld " Mailie " he'd a tear
To shed beside her mountain bier ;
He ca'd the sheep frae far an' near,
　　　　　　　Wi' grief to wrestle ;
But " Mailie " was beyont the fear
　　　　　　　Of butcher's trestle.

And een the wee an' tremblin mousie,
He wouldna' rob of its bit housie.
He made that crawlin pest, the ——,
     A judge o' fashions :
An' gave to it, sae prim an' doucie,
     A critic's notions.

Wha kens wha Rabbie might ha been,
If life a longer lease had gi'en ?
Yet ere he left this earthly scene,
     For Death's dark portal,
A simple flower* o' modest mien,
     He'd made immortal.

* The Daisy.

LAMENT FOR THE FAILSWORTH
"POLE."

This ancient landmark, so well known throughout the country,
has been taken down, as it was deemed unsafe on account of decay.
"Ab" overhears the wail of the wooden relic on his return one
evening from the "Old Bell."—*Manchester Guardian*.

THEY'VE ta'en me down at last, theau sees,
    Becose I'm gettin rotten,
An' that's no wonder when I think
    I've been so long forgotten.

There's nob'dy tricked me caut wi' paint,
    Nor trimmed my vane an' points,
Nor weshed my face, nor combed my yure,
    Nor oiled my creakin joints,

Sin' I're put here to face the storm,
    An' wintry frosts an' snows :
An' not a drop o' comfort sent
    To thaw my frozen nose.

It wurno so when th' lord o'th' lond
    Wi' ribbons decked by yead,
An' made me change my politics
    By turnin blue to red.

I wonder what th' " Owd Ship " would say,
    An' " Trumpet-foot " would do,
If they could rise before their time,
    An' see what I've come to ?

Th' owd " smith* " would make his anvil ring,
　　An' eke his bellows blow,
If he wur towd th' " V.R." wur gone
　　He'd fashioned years ago.

An' chanticleer has left his perch,
　　Becose he're eaut o' place ;
To stond wi' th' creawn beneath his tail
　　He felt wur a disgrace.

So long as we'n a Queen to rule
　　The fates of fowls an' men,
An' show us th' way eaur feelins blow,
　　It owt t' ha' been a hen.

Farewell, owd bird! an' when I'm gone
　　To join the shades o' men,
They'll wish they'd spared a bit o' paint
　　To mak me young again.

But neaw another'll tak my place,
　　A masher for a time,
But he'll come deawn to rust and chips
　　Before he's past his prime.

So 'tis wi' men as weel as pows,
　　Neglected i' their day ;
An' when they're come to coffin dust
　　They'll find a bed o' clay.

---

　　* Local Celebrities of the past.

THE STONEBREAKER'S SONG.

It was a study to see him at work. Seated on a wisp of hay that he had twisted and coiled into a cushion ; a girdle of the same material laid on a large flat-surfaced stone in front of him ; a large hammer laid by his side, and in his hand a smaller one, with which he would now and then peg away, as if in the act of breaking Jacobins' heads by the score ; a visor of wire-cloth suspended over his face, to prevent splinters of stone from flying into his eyes ; an old blue jacket, that at one time had been a coat, looped over a red plush " singlet " of perhaps twenty or even forty years' wear : his almost hairless sconce bared to the sun, from which it had received an imperishable coating of tan, he was an object that few would pass without hailing with observations, either concerning the weather, or the crops or the idle gossip of the time.

Strange! This Sunday morning the old fellow was at *work*—busily, merrily at work. The church bells seemed to swing in time to the song he was trolling ; and the lark that would poise itself over the patch of wrinkled tan as if it had been a note-book, sang in a strain that made the hammer quicken in its descent ; and the splinters of stone would be threshed out of the girdle till the tawny patch would be as pearled over with dew as were the fields around. Suddenly he paused to take wind. He wiped his shining sconce with a tattered napkin, and raised his visor to look about him. How still and serene and Sabbath-like were the old road-mender's reflections, as he contemplated the quiet and sunny landscape before him—" meetly " Sabbath-like !—and he listened to the bells again.

" What is ther up at th' church this mornin !" he asked himself, wiping his face, and listening again. " Is some foo or other gettin wed, I wonder ? Ay, I dar'say ; ther's aulus someb'dy thinkin they con mend other folk's wark ; it's th' natur of a foo." And down

went the visor with a jerk ; "click" went the hammer, and showers
of splinters flew out of the girdle as he sang—

Young Robin at th' smithy a-cooarten did go,
With his heigh smithy ballis an' anvil an' o!
He wur one score an' nothin, just th' age for a foo',
But owder wur Kit by a haytime or two.
                    Singin derry down, Robin.
                    No sighin nor sobbin
W'll e'er tee a love-knot 'tween Kitty an' thee.

Neaw Robin he begged, as he stood i'th' heause porch,
Ut Kitty ud let him just tak her to th' church ;
But Kitty said, "Nawe, lad, no church yet for me ;
For a yer or two lunger aw meean to be free."
                    Singin derry down, ditty,
                    A snicket wur Kitty ;
Her heart wur as hard as a weightstone, aw'm sure.

"He should ha' gan her a whizz i'th earhole, an' axed her how
hoo liked that," commented the singer, raising his hammer and
bringing it down with a force that made more fragments than were
intended. "Nowt like a good hommerin for a saucy besom ut
wants so—husk!—so mich trouble makkin on her," and again the
stones flew out of the girdle, and again the road-mender took up
the strain—

Her lover had waited a twelvemonth or more,
An' neetly he'd striven her heart to get o'er ;
But seein at last ut hoo laafed as he spoke,
His pluck dropt so low ut he're ready to choke.
                    Singin derry down, Robin,
                    Theau's done to mich sobbin,
Cock thi hat o' one side, an' goo whistlin whoam.

"Aw'll see thee once moore," young Robin he said,
,'An' ax thee agen if theau means to be wed;
An' if theau says *nawe*, theau may go to th' *owd lad*,
For Margit o' Peter's is toyert of her dad."

Singin bravely spoke, Robin,
That's better nor sobbin;
Hoo'll smile no moore yet at th' breet side ov her een.

" Ay, that trick onswers sometimes. Try some other wench on
—someb'dy they care no' mich about. It'll be as straight forrad as
hay makkin i' good sun and wynt. Then th' tother 'll come round
like midsummer, or a rent day ; an' be as whinin an' as fain as a
new-byetten hound. Ay, ay; better nor churnin ee-wayter, an'
pooin a face as long an' as feaw as a milestone ut's had smo'-pox."

Next time he went armed wi' a peawer he'd ne'er tried,
An' owd oak back-spittle* he'd slung by his side,
Ut wur chalked o'er wi *X's*, hauve moon's an' reaund *O's*,
Wi' a lot o' straight strokes ut wur set caut i' rows.

Singin derry down, Robin,
Theau's entered a job in
Ut'll be murder to Kitty, an' hangin to thee.

" Owd Nanny i'th' fowt used to reckon up her shop-scores o'
that fashion. A *X* stood for a farthin ; a *straight stroke* for a penny ;
a *hauve moon* for a sixpence, and a reaund *O* for a shillin. Hoo'd
every inch o' wood i'th' shop chalked o'er once for brass ut wur
owin ; an' when ther nowt else ut 'ud howd a figger hoo began o'
scorin upo' their Ned's back, till lads abeaut coed him th' walkin
shopbook."

"Well, does theau say *nawe* yet?" young Robin he said.
Kitty made him no onswer, but threw up her yed.
"Then look here at this—pay me o ut theau owes."
An' he flourished th' owd back-spittle under her nose.

Singin derry down, ditty,
A floorer for Kitty,
Wur th' *X's*, *straight strokes*, an' *reaund O's*, an' *hauve moons*.

"He should ha' laid it on her back till her stays ud ha' skriked
out. *I* would ha' done."

" This is what aw wore on thee last yer," Robin cried,
" For a fippunny pincushion t' hang bi thi side ;
Two link of a necklace, a pin for thi gown
An a new fleawred huzziff aw breawt eaut o'th' teawn."

                Singin derry down, Robin,
                Theau's set Kit a-sobbin ;
Theau'll have her i' fits if theau reads any moore.

" Then aw I took thee to th' fair," Robin said with a sigh,
" An' bowt thee some nuts an' a gingybread pie ;
Some porter aw paid for at th' ' Skewer an' Cop,'
An' two caunces o' towfy at owd Nanny's shop."

                Singin derry down, Kitty,
                Thy Robin's no pity.
Or else he'd wipe th' score off an' set thi bont free.

   " Th' next byets cock-feightin."

Kitty sighed, and said " Robin, aw'll pay thee thi shot ;
Wilt have it i' money, or papper, or what ?"
But, before he could spake hoo'd her arm reaund his neck,
An' th' owd oak back-spittle were wiped to a speck.

                Singin derry down, ditty,
                Neaw Robin an' Kitty
Han chalked up a score ut'll last 'em for life.

TO EDWIN WAUGH.

The writer had not heard from his poetical friend for a considerable time. The circumstance suggested this epistle, which
Mr. Waugh included in an edition of his own poems.

WHAT ails thee, Ned ? Thour't not as 'twur,
　　Or else no' what I took thee for,
When fust thou made sich noise an' stir
　　　　　I' this quare pleck.
Hast' flown at Fame wi' sich a ber,
　　　　　As t' break thy neck ?

Or arta droppin' fithers, eh ;
An' keepin' th' neest warm till some day,
Toart April-tide, or sunny May,
　　　　　When thou may'st spring,
An' warble out a new-made lay,
　　　　　On strengthened wing ?

For brids o' sung mun ha' ther mou't,
As weel as other brids I doubt ;
But though they peearch beneath a spout,
　　　　　Or roost 'mong heather,
They're saved fro' mony a shiverin' bout,
　　　　　By hutchin' t'gether.

D

Come, let owd Mother Dumps a-be,
An' wag thy yead wi' friendly glee;
Fly o'er, a humble brid to see—
   This wo'ld is wide—
There's reaum for booath thee an' me,
   An' more beside.

Come, scrat' thy bill, an' bat thy wings;
Hark how the merry " Layrock " sings !
Good news fro' flowerlond he brings
   In his glad throat ;
An' conno' thou, 'mong lesser things,
   Put in a note ?

The buds that peep fro' every spray ;
The cock that wakkens up the day ;
The thrush that sings its roundelay
   I' bower an' tree,
Shout—" Come, owd brid, an' have a say
   I' nature's spree !"

For 'tis a spree, this life o' ours ;
Drinkin' wine fro' cups o' flowers,
An' takkin' insence in i' showers,
   Enoogh to crack us;
Or havin' glorious neetly cowers
   Wi' a fithered Bacchus.

Fly o'er thysel, or if thou chooses
To bring some other brids o' th' Muses,
Pike out a flock, an' come an' rooze this,
   My peearchin cote ;
The mou't seize him who then refuses
   To tune his throat.

Foremost in flight, on gentle wing,
The " Prestwich Philomela " [1] bring.
It swells my crop to yer him sing,
   I' plaintive strain ;
To squeeze his claw wi' friendly wring
   I would be fain.

Then ther's that owd gray-toppined lark,
Who sang when thou an' I wur dark,
Long years sin', o'er toart th' " Little Park,"
   " Bamford " [2] his name ;
Let's give our yeads a reverent jark,
   An' own his fame.

Bring in thy train thoose brids o' note,
Blithe " Charlie," [3] with his wattled throat,
An' " Dick," [4] who never sang nor wrote
   To hurt his fellow ;
With him, [5] who aye wi' " seed-box " sote
   To mak' brids mellow.

Bring him who to the Past still clings, [6]
Who in some moss-grown ruin sings,
Whilst delvin' deep for bygone things
   I' tombs an' ditches ;
Now croonin' o'er the deeds o' kings,
   Or pranks o' witches.

2 Samuel Bamford; author of " Passages in the Life of a
Radical," &c.
 3 Charles Hardwick; author of " The History of Preston," &c
 4 R. R. Bealey ; author of " After Business Jottings," &c.
 5 Joseph Chatwood, President of the Manchester Literary Club.
 6 John Harland; Editor of " Baine's History of Lancashire,"
             &c.

An' bring that honest soul thy skoo' in,[7]
Who *notes* what other birds are dooin' :
Who at a "weed' is aules pooin',
   To sweel his throttle ;
Who if he's mute is surely brewin'
   Some genial prattle.

An' bring that grizzly weazent wren,[8]
Who twitters nobbut now an' then ;
Who " ale " prescribes to " physic " men,
   An' brids as weel.
(If souls obeyed his guidin' ken,
   They'd starve the de'il.)

An' to mak' up the festive cage,
Bring that plump brid, the " Happy Page :"
Who'd give in song the exact gauge
   Of throat o' viper, [10]
An' tell, by countin' fithers, th' age
   O' woodland piper.

Wi' hop an' twitter, chirp an' sung,
We'd drive the scamperin' hours alung ;
An' it thy glee, an' 'Lijah's lung,
   I' tone should slacken,
Ther'd be enoogh o' Charlie's tongue
   To keep us wakken.

---

7 J. P. Stokes, Esq., Correspondent of the *Times*.

8 Elijah Ridings ; author of the " Village Muse," &c.

9 John Page (Felix Folio); author of " Street Dealers and Quacks," &c.

10 Mr. Page, in " Letters on Natural History," maintains that the viper, in time of danger, swallows its young.

We'd ha' " Tim's Grave,"an " Th' Sweetheart Gate,"
An' "Owd Pegge's " cure for th' wakkerin' state ;[11]
An " Jerry,"[12] too, should shake his pate
      Wi' monkey claiver ;
An' if yo'rn short o' rhymin prate,
      I'd croon " Th' Owd Wayver."

We mit o' love an' friendship sing ;
O' Charity's exhaustless spring ;
O' Beauty, that wi' radiant wing,
      Charms brid and bard ;
An' then, for th' sake o'th' fun 'twould bring,
      Try th' jokin' " card."[13]

A neet o' sich like mirthfu' croozin',
No friend forgettin'—no foe abusin';
Now leaud i' sung, now sweetly musin',
      Were " bliss divine ;"
An' to the soul a deep infusin'
      O' Jove's best wine.

Thus may we flutter through life's grove,
Now crack't wi' glee, now steeped i' love,
Till wingin' to that roost above,
      Where dwell the blest,
We find, like Noah's faithful dove,
      A place o' rest.

---

11 *Vide* " Ale *versus* Physic," by Elijah Ridings.

12 Alluding to a humorous story about a " monkey," told with considerable gusto by Charles Hardwick.

13 A term much used in conversstion by one of the worthies above named.

On Attaining His 70th Year, January 29th, 1887.

'Tis over thirty years, friend Waugh,
　　Since thou and I first met.
A manly face, a twinkling eye,
　　A voice to music set,

Were thine to please, to charm, to win,
　　All round the social board,
Where kindly sympathetic ears
　　Hung on each tuneful word.

Since then I've roamed the moorland wild,
　　With poesy and thee;
And pressed the fragrant heather bell
　　With footstep light and free.

And I have known thee since, when care
　　And dire affliction traced
The lines that tell of weary days
　　No healing hath effaced—

When silver crept amongst thy hair,
　　Now changed to wintry rime:
And stooped thy form beneath the load
　　Of unrelenting Time.

Thy lyre hath sounded mid the strife
　　Of worldly thoughts and ways;
Thy song hath cheered the helpless wight,
　　With dreams of happier days.

Soon thou must lay thy harp aside,
  Hushed for the passing hour ;
But Memory may wake its tones
  With echoes of its power.

The sun of thy poetic day
  For ever may have set ;
But rosy are the twilight tints
  That linger round thee yet.

Ere these dissolve in darksome night,
  And leave thy soul forlorn,
May'st thou behold the breaking light
  Of an eternal morn.

THOSE TOWN HALL STAIRS.

MAIDEN SPEECH

Delivered in the Manchester City Council, May 3, 1876, on the question locating the Free Reference Library in the upper rooms of the New Town Hall.

In November, 1875, Mr. Brierley was elected a city councillor, and his maiden speech was in support of the Free Libraries Committee's successful attempt to prevent the reference department being located in the attic of the Town Hall. Here was his opportunity. The chairman of the Free Libraries Committee, Mr. Alderman (afterwards Sir Thomas) Baker, said, addressing Mr. Brierley, ' We shall want all the help we can get, see what you can do.' On the day fixed for the debate, Mr. Brierley rose and said— ' He felt that to place a vast collection of literary treasures out of the reach of many for whom they were got together would be legislating backwards, unless it were the desire of the Corporation to preserve them as some country dames did their copper kettles, by never allowing them to be made use of. (Laughter.) Great stress had been laid, but mostly inside the Council, upon the cost of an independent structure erected in a central part of the city. Whoever brought that argument forward as an objection to a general scheme forgot the importance of the institution sought to be located, and the great value set upon such institutions by our neighbours across the Channel. A North Country friend of his, describing the extent and splendour of the temples devoted to the arts, the sciences, and the literature of a nation, to be met with in even the smaller cities of continental Europe, and comparing them with our own, observed—' Why, mon, we're not in it at a'.' (Laughter.) He told the truth, we are *not* in it. (Hear, hear.) When a few months ago the Watch Committee asked the Council for an additional £40,000 to enlarge an already palatial residence for our criminal population, not a murmur was raised against the demand. But when they asked that a powerful instrument for preventing crime might be properly and not extravagantly housed, they were told that an attic in the new Town Hall was quite good enough for the purpose. And what was this retreat, or sepulchre, for the great minds of the world? To paraphrase a favourite couplet of Mr. Fox Turner's —

I have been there, but would not go
Again, I'd rather stay below.

(Laughter.) Independent of other considerations, a library of reference was of little service unless it were of ready access; and locating it at an altitude that could not be reached without having to climb steps to the number of 120, would be like placing a piece of bread on a dog's nose, and counting 120 before allowing it to be snapped up. (Loud laughter.) His experience of this part of the building had more than confirmed, if possible, the opinions he had always held as to its unsuitableness for any important purpose whatever. A few weeks ago he had been one of an expedition that had volunteered to explore the mysterious regions of the carillons, and the conclusion he then came to was, that none but such adventurous spirits as the Mayor and Mr. Alderman Heywood would ever have the hardihood to climb that giddy height. (Laughter.) The whole party commenced the ascent of the stairs at the same time, but like amateur mountaineers climbing Ben Lomond, they gradually became separated—some hanging on here and there by a balustrade, and others trying to emulate the pranks of their boyish days by a grotesque attempt to look nimble. (Laughter.) By dint of dogged perseverance they all reached the top, but not in a body. They turned up in panting and perspiring driblets (laughter), the last man being a little over ten minutes behind his immediate predecessor. (Renewed Laughter.) He would not repeat the expression this laggard made use of on landing, but would describe it as an empathic kind of thinking aloud. (Laughter.) If, then, such difficulties presented themselves to the active and energetic members of the City Council, what would they be to men of more than ordinary bulk, and when getting into years? Only imagine an elderly man of fifteen stone spending half an hour in worming himself up this crenated corkscrew for the purpose of ascertaining at what period of the world's history Manchester was besieged by the Shandeans. (Laughter.) He imagined it to be some such possibility that gave the idea for the construction of a piece of doggrel that had recently come under his notice. Whether it be from the pen of Long-Short-or-any-other-fellow he would leave them to surmise when they had given it the favour of a hearing. It was as follows:—

The shades of night were falling fast,
As up the Town Hall steps there passed,
A man who on his shoulders bore
Full seventy winters,—and he swore—
    " These cursed stairs!"

Firmly he grasped an alpenstock,
To help his legs from block to block;

And as he toiled his way along,
Throughout each corridor there rang—
    " Confound these stairs ! "

From warehouse window came no light,
Which could illume that misty height ;
And when he found himself alone,
From out his breast escaped a groan—
    " These Town Hall stairs ! "

" Wither goest thou ? " a porter said,
With buttons on his coat o'erspread.
" I go to con historic lore ;
But clamber up I'll never more
    These Town Hall stairs ! "

A maiden old, with features brown,
The balusters was cleaning down ;
And as the pilgrim raised his head,
Half frightened at the sight she said—
    " Oh, drat these stairs."

Rough was the night, the storm without
A torrent made in lead and spout,
And rattled 'gainst the window pane,
That none could hear the echo, vain—
    " Where are the stairs ? "

At early morn, as duty-ward
The porters trod the pavement hard,
They heard a voice call from on high,
As if 'twere shouted from the sky—
    " Where are the stairs ? "

There on the cold mosiac. lay
The old man bent, and worn, and grey.
He'd been locked in ; and as he grasped
An Alpenstock, he faintly gasped—
     " These Town Hall stairs ! "

Ye who of Helicon have quaffed,
And studied till you're nearly daft,
Is this the watchword of your craft
You'd shout along that spiral shaft—
     " Excelsior ? "

Oh ! what would Grundy say. or Lamb,
If without aid of 'bus or tram.
They'd thus to climb, their heads to cram ?
" All right, Excelsior, but d——
     These Town Hall stairs ! "

The reading of these verses caused much merriment, and Mr.
Brierley sat down amid shouts of laughter and cheers.

" Mr. Alderman Lamb said he must confess that it required
one to be possessed of considerable nerve who rose to speak after
what they had just heard from the new councillor, &c., &c.

" The report was adopted by a large majority.

" When the council rose Mr. Alderman Baker, slapping Mr.
Brierley on the shoulder, said—'You've settled the question. No
other man in the council could have done it.'

" Thus, an uneducated weaver, almost fresh from the loom,
had to champion the cause of the learned societies of Manchester,
a service that has not yet been acknowledged. Mr. Brierley had
made his mark as a councillor.

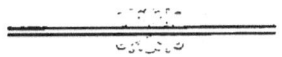

EPILOGUE,

*Delivered on the occasion of closing the Oldham Exhibition,
January 5th, 1884.*

NOW does the engine end its busy run,
    Rake out its fires, and say its work is done.
No more its throbbings, scarcely heard or felt,
Shall send pulsations through each cord and belt—
But like a giant whose journey's at it's close,
Lays down its limbs, and seeks well-earned repose.
No more we'll listen to the throstle's song,—
Not the wild notes we hear when days are long,
But more like hum of bee when at its toil,
(I think my Muse requires a little oil.)
No more we'll watch the steady pace of mule,—
Not the queer animal from Balaam's school—
But from that stud erst vitalised by Watt,
And given shape and motion by a Platt.
No more we'll see Niagara from a pump,
Nor feel old times renewed in " double bump,"
No more the rattle of the busy loom
Shall ears assail, as 'twere the tongue of doom.
No more we'll watch with wondering regards
Grow line by line the sharp and bristling cards,—

I do not mean those square and painted things,
On which we see quaint forms of queens and kings,—
With which sometimes we're skinned to the last
    "rap,"
By joining in a friendly game at "nap"—
But cards to comb with, as we comb our hair,—
Not as our wives do with a stool or chair.
No more we'll see how without wheels, or cranks,
They weave a worsted covering for our shanks ;
Nor feel as if some danger near might lurk,
By seeing the "devil" (printers') at his work.
No more we'll see the "masher" at the bar,
Ord'ring his B. and S., and a cigar,
Whilst "Hebe," with Skye terrier fringe or "bang,"
Smiles as she listens to his pretty slang.
Gone are the visions, or shall soon depart,
Of those creations struck from the mould of art :—
The painted canvass, or the sculptured form,—
The peaceful landscape, and old ocean's storm.
To things that touch the soul, and charm the eye
We now must bid a lingering good-bye.
No, not to all, thanks to the "Rough-head's" pluck.—
(The envious might say 'twas only luck)—
Some things of beauty will remain to be
A joy for aye—a life's eternity.
Who would have thought the time would ever come
When Art in Oldham would have found a home ?
Yet here she is, well housed, and clothed, and fed ;
To Industry allied, to Science wed.
But now for words I'm getting sorely pressed,—
So mote it be ! the Mayor will do the rest.

JOHNNY OVER THE SALT SEA.

(Betty-o'er-th'-lone's song in the "Layrock of Langleyside.")

IT was down by yonder river side
    Where cat-tails they do grow,
I met a pretty fair maid
    With bosom white as snow,
I said, my pretty maiden fair,
    My dearest love, said I,
Wilt thou be mine in sweet wedlock ?
    Come answer me proper*ly*.

She blushed and took from off her neck,
    From off her neck she took,
A ribbon fair tied with a bow,
    And then gave me a look.
She said, you see this ribbon fair,
    This ribbon fair you see ;
Oh, I prize it more than silver or gold,
    For my true-love gave it me.

My Johnny's gone o'er the salt sea
   On board of a man-of-war,
And letters I get every month
   From my true-hearted tar.
Don't think that I would him deceive,
   Who constant thus hath been ;
But I said, my dear, I'll soon settle that,
   Your Johnny I have seen.

She fainted straight into my arms
   At the mention of Johnny's name ;
Then said, oh, tell me, is he still,
   Oh, is he still the same ?
I said he'd married a black-a-moor,
   All in East Indi-a ;
And he would never come to England more
   Across the wide salt sea.

This maiden then the ribbon took
   All by that cat-tailed river,
And threw as far as she could throw
   The keepsake of her lover ;
She said, kind sir, your wife I'll be,
   If you'll be true to me,
And I never will think of Johnny more,
   All over the salt sea.

LINES

Addressed by Sam Laycock to the "Failsworth
Gathering," March 29th.

OLD friends of Ben Brierley, I'm sure your are right
  In promoting this praisworthy gathering to-night ;
And all thoughtful right-minded men will approve
Of the spirit displayed in the " labour of love ;"
So it seems that the country is wakening at last
To the errors our forefathers made in the past.
Namely, treating their bees as no better than drones,
And, when dead, raising monuments over their bones ;
They neglected the tune till the player was mute,
Then all they could do was to honour the flute.
Well, now, friends, I think I may venture to say
Than in matters like this we are wiser to-day ;
And, if we may judge from this gathering to-night,
The outlook for authors is getting more bright.
I feel proud of this meeting ; like good men and true.
You give honour to one to whom honour is due ;
For while London reared Dickens, and others as great,
It was Failsworth that reared the renowned Ab-o'th'-Yate.
It was here the weaver lad spent his young days,
And here as a man composed his first lays ;

And it seems only natural, and fitting, that now,
When age and the deep lines of care mark his brow,
You should honour the bard with his silvery hairs,
And as far as you can do so—lighten his cares ;
And authors have cares, there is not the least doubt,
Yes, cares that the world can know little about,
For have you not read of " Wearisome toil,"
In some attic, aloft, burning " midnight oil,"
And nothing on earth seems more certain or sure,
Than this well-known fact that " all poets are poor."
Well, who is to blame, then, for this state of things
The people who hear, or the singer who sings ?
Which needs the most effort ? let this be the test,
And then common sense will decide all the rest.
But the feeling that seems to be current to day,
Is to give those who need it " a lift on the way ;"
I honour Tom Nash, with his warm manly heart,
For taking so noble and active a part.
And to my mind it greatly enhances the deed,
When we take in account his political creed.
It shows that the bard is esteemed for his worth,
Irrespective of politics, favour or birth.
I should like to be with you to show the regard
That I have for my genial and famed brother bard ;
But this must not be, so I cannot do less
Than wish that your meeting may prove a success.
God bless "Ab-o'th'-Yate" in his basket and store,
And when he lands safe on Columbian's shore,
May he meet with kind friends, true in heart and in hand
As those he will leave in his own native land.

E

JONE O' GRINFILT'S GHOST.

I 'RE sitting one neet in my owd two-armed chair,
    Wi' my feet upo' th' fender—my nose cocked i'th'
       air ;
When I thowt I smelt summat like matches ablaze,
Then a hont cowd as ice coom an' felt at my face.
        Thinks I —Am I wick ;
        Or is this chap Owd Nick,
    Comn a fotchin me deawn to his whoam.

Yo'r sure I're weel waken't an, gloppent wi' th' shock ;
I groped o reawnd th' hearthstone, an' felt up at th'
       clock ;
Peeped under th' couch-cheear, an'th' table i'th' nook ;
Felt abeawt th' chimdy bottom, an' struck th' rack'an-
       hook ;
        But nowt could I feel
        Ut wur owt like the di'el,
    Nor see what I couldno' mak eawt.

So I seete deawn agen an' kept lookin' o reawnd ;
But nowt could I see, an' could yer not a seawnd,
Till th' clock dinged eawt *ten*, an' then—eh, what a seet!
Ther summat crept past in a blaze o' blue leet.
        I hutcht i' mi hoide,
        An' could hardly aboide
    To look wheere it seete itsel' deawn.

I said—" Mesther Sooty, if that's what yo'r co'ed,
What maks you come here, so far cawt o' yo'r road ?
I'd ha' thowt ther moore pikin' i' Lunnon nor here,
For ther's lots o' fat sinners I'm towd liven theer."

  Th' owd lad he ne'er stir'd,
  An' he spoke not a word,
 But kept sittin' an' starin' at me.

When he gleawert awhile wi' a look quite as keen
As the bore of a gimlet, he twinkled his een ;
An' his face looked so mich like a face ut I'd known,
Ut I couldno' help sheawtin'—" By gad, it's Owd Jone !"

  He said—" Dody Kicker,—
  Heaw arta for liquor ?
 It's dry wheere I come fro' theaw'rt sure.

" I've chew'd coffin lids till my teeth are like saws,
An' gravestones are rayther too hard for my jaws ;
Hast getten owt better, if nobbut a snack ;
For digesshun's noane good when one's laid o' ther
  back.

  So bring out thy table,
  And get what theaw'rt able,—
 I'm wambly wi' trudgin' so far."

I said—" If that's thee, theaw'st ha' th' best I con
   ,bring ;
But times are so bad sin' we geet a new king ;
I've nowt nobbut wayther just drawn caut o'th' well,
An' a cob o breawn jannock I'd saved for mysel'.

  Theaw'rt welcome to feed on't,
  If mayte theaw has need on't,
 An' I'll whistle for th' next ut'll come."

Owd Jone shaked his noddle, and felt at his chin—
" Bring it out then " he said, "for I long to begin,
Dost no' think theaw con get me a drop o *maut tac :*
For wayther's a bad thing for keepin' one's clay.
   A drop o good toddy's
   A comfort for bodies,
  Whether livin' or laid into the ground."

" Just wait thee a minnit," I said, an' I'll goo
An' see if Owd Mall has a sope o' th' last brew ;
Put thy hont into th' cubbart an' tak' what ther' is ;
If theaw's had nowt but coffins theaw'll do noan amiss."
   So wi' th' jug cawt I sallies,
   An' runs to Owd Mally's,
  An' gets it brim full o' breawn ale.

When I geet back to th' heawse Jone wur wipin' his
  lips ;
He seemed to think *jannock* wur better than *chips.*
" Gie me howd o' that pitcher," he said, an' let's drink;
Yo're no' mich better off nor what *we* are, I think.
   O' th' jannock, to be sure,
   I could do wi' some moore ;
  But th' *beef* wur o' *gristle* I'll swear."

Wi' that he swiped th' ale up, and looked into th' pot,
Took his neetcap an' crutches, an' said he must trot ;
But what he used th' sticks for I never could tell,
For he dropt straight through th' floor an'—left *me* by
  mysel.
   Then wonnerin' an' starin',
   Thinks I, theaw'rt a quare un,
  If *beef* theaw could find where ther' noane.

I struck up a leet, for neaw th' heawse wur o' dark,
An' I skeawlt deawn at th' floor, but I fund not a mark ;
When at the table I looked—theer wur th' *heels o' mi shoon*,
Ut I'd just stumpt wi' hobnails an' put upo' th' oon.

   An' heaw *jannock* an' *leather*
   Ud mix up together,
  Owd Jone happen knows afore neaw.

MORAL.

A moral, I'm sure, yo' con see i' this sung ;
It may ha' bin taydious, it may ha' bin lung ;
But o' this ther's no deawt, that heaw hungry one feels,
There are others wur off if they'n tackle *shoon heels ;*

   So let's give o'er sighin'
   An' grumblin' an' cryin',
  An' try to do th' best ut we con.

BATHING.

(Not after Thomson.)

THE sea hove gently, frilled with tiny waves,
    That shimmered on the beach, or crept in
        caves,—
As if, with infant breezes, raised to show
How liquid smiles o'er Ocean's face may flow.

And their soft kisses fell on tide-borne limbs—
Fair as the Oceanides of old ;
And favoured wavelets wantoned with the threads
Of unbound tresses— ravelled webs of gold,—

When Damon, idly strolling on the shore,
His hands within his pockets, turning o'er
The friendly coins, hears Musidora's voice—
" Eh, Mary, do come in,—it is so noice !"

The youth turns round, beholds the straggling vans
Dipping their thirsty axles in the wave ;
And, by a green one, numbered " 23,"
A timid nymph her shivering form doth lave.

It is his Musidora ; he had missed
Her from the pier an hour ago, but wist
Not that she'd laid aside her prudish ways,
In azure sack to court the vulgar gaze.

Her hair about her shoulders floateth free ;
(The bunch that held her hat sublimely poised
Upon her burthened head, in van is stored,—
'Twas bought in Manchester, and's highly prized).

And now she's gone,—the waves meet where she
    stood :
" Oh, that I were the sea, or some such flood !"
The youth exclaims. Again he hears the voice—
" Eh, Mary, do come in,—it is so noice !"

The two had come from Oldham, *via* trips
By speculative gentlemen got up,
To gather shells, ride " donks," and see the ships ;
Then home return, on prawns and shrimps to sup.

And there were other nymphs within the van,
Yclept Mary, Sally, and Selina Ann ;
The three were getting ready for a dash
Into the briny billow, there to—splash.

Anon a timid foot steps down the stair—
'Tis Mary's. Shrinking from a wave, whose lip
Hath kissed her ankle, she in fear exclaims--
" Eh, Bet, I wish I're back again wi' th' trip !"

But Sal, less timid, ventures down behind,
And, with a push more vigorous than kind,
Poor Mary sends adrift ; then plunging in
Herself, a war of splashing doth begin.

Whilst Musidora, vulgarly called " Bet,"
In swimming attitude cleaves wave 'yond wave ;
Tracing a line of foam, as with *one* foot
(The other *hopping*) she the tide doth brave.

The battle rages near ; Selina Ann
Hath scarcely left the threshold of the van
Ere she is " ducked," and held a moment down,
Whilst Sally's head is yet dry at the crown.

Then booms a thundering shout along the shore-
" Duck th' big un, lasses ! " meaning Sal the bold,
And Sal is seized, and made to kiss the sand
And promise quarter ere they loose their hold.

Now all go down ; the bubbling waves close o'er—
Then comes a whistle from the far-off shore ;—
The train is starting ; Damon, franctic tries
To stop it—vain attempt—yet on he flies.

The others scream and toss their arms on high ;
Their sack-encumbered limbs divide the spray,
Then to the privacy of " 23 "
The dripping mermaids mount the laddered way.

The train is gone, and with it Damon too ;
Ah, why to Musidora so untrue?
And why leave Mary and Selina Ann
With Sal to quarrel in that cursed van ?

When rose the moon upon the tranquil beach–
(The sun had got his nightcap on, and lay
As if in cradled slumber) from a bank
Four weeping fair ones watched the closing day.

The night set in ; the midwatch came and went ;
The god of morn his golden iris bent
O'er eastern wave; yet these four maidens slept
Upon the bank where they had watched and wept.

And now the tale is told in Oldham town,
How Musidora Damon's letters tore ;
And by next trip to " pool," or " port," went down.
And strewed the fragments on th' avenging shore.

CELIA.

COLIN.   Where art thou, CELIA, idol of my heart!
        Thou lovely truant from my bleating
           fold?
        Art thou a-hide-and-seeking in the grove,
          Or gathering bilberries on the tangled
           wold?

[" CELIA " who is more frequently called " Sally," and who does not tend sheep, hears not her COLIN's invocation; but leaning against the posts of the kitchen-door, is listening to the commonplace wooing of a less poetic rival. This youth, whom vulgar people call " JOE o' JUDDIE's," but whom poets would perhaps have named " Celadon," is plying his importunities with commendable zeal; and the heart of the maiden being but a *woman's*, and held to be as unimpressible as stone, inclineth her ear to listen. But she has not yielded as yet; and COLIN's voice is again making the woods musical with plaintive invocation]

COLIN.   Vainly, my CELIA, have I searched each
                bower
            Where oft in happier moments thou hast
                been ;
            As fruitlessly have I the moorland swept ;
            Thou wert not there, nor elsewhere to be
                seen.

CELADON (*to Celia*).—Well, if theau's made up thy
mind for t' ha' yon po'try-writing leatheryead, I'll shift
my shanks eaut o' this cote. But before I goo let me
tell thee ut I've brass i' th' bank.

CELIA.—So has Robin (*meaning* COLIN).

CELADON.—I've won a pig in a raffle, an' when it's
ready for killin' I'se sell it, an' buy a keaw.

CELIA.—Robin has a keaw o ready an' two shares in
a buildin' club.

[CELADON is silent, and COLIN resumes the duties of
poetical bellman.]

COLIN.   The orb of light is not more true to earth ;
            The seasons not more constant in their
                run ;
            The magnet looks not with less wavering
                point
            Polewards, than I to thee, my lovely one !

CELADON (*making another spurt*).—I'll buy thee a new
bonnet if theau'll give yond mon up, an' tee thysel to me.

CELIA.—My mother's promised me one against th'
wakes.

CELADON.—A new frock, then,

CELIA.—I've one i' makkin' neaw.

[CELADON is again at his whit's end for an accept-
able " votive offering," and applies himself to a
primitive mode of hair-dressing to help him over
the difficulty. The sylvan-crier still prosecutes
his inquiries.]

COLIN. Then say, my CELIA, why from me dost hide ?
　　　Why rack thy COLIN's breast with doubt
　　　　　and pain ?
　　　Is it for CELADON thy heart's reserved ?
　　　Say, faithless maiden, have I loved in
　　　　　vain ?

CELADON (*who begins to suspect he has been going on the
wrong tack, strikes out a new course*).—Am I too quiet for
thee, as theau howds out so lung ? Becose, if I am, I
con be a bit different. I con leather Bob any day if it
comes to a tussle. Look at that, neaw. (*Raises a
mountain of muscle on his right arm*). Ther's some
peawer theere. I con throw two fifty-sixes o'er my
yead at once.

CELIA.—Theau conno lift me up wi' one arm.

CELADON.—Connot I ? We'n see whether I con or
not. (*Takes hold of CELIA by the waist, and raises her from
her feet. CELIA utters a faint scream.*)

COLIN. The hour is past when I was wont to see
　　　Thy sylph-like form appear beyond the
　　　　　gate ;

The poultry roostward pick their noiseless
way,
And still thou art not here.   Oh, why so
late ?
Ah, now I see what's kept thee from my
arms !
That viper, CELADON, has stopt the way.
Now farewell, Muse !—Come Mars with
vengeful steel,
And help my triumph in the coming fray !

[*Strangely enough, CELADON, whilst in the act of testing
the weight of his inamorata, somehow manages to bring the
tip of his nose into close proximity with that of CELIA'S.
They pass each other ; return : pass and return again : a
smacking sound following, which evidently is only too delightful
not to repeat.   This weighing operation seals the fate of the
poetic suitor, who arrives on the scene just as his rival is in the
act of trying the strength of his left arm.   Their clogs meet ;
but the maiden decides in favour of CELADON : and COLIN
takes to a new mistress, and a more successful method of wooing.*]

For " steel " read " clogs."

JOHNNY AN' PEGGY.

" IT'S two score year an' ten, owd lass,
    Sin' fust I coorted thee ;
Yo' lived that time at Katty Green,
    At top o' Bowman's Lea.

" I'd seen thee trip through Coppie Wood ;
    I'd met thee at the steel ;
But when I tried to spake to thee,
    Heaw quare my heart did feel !

" A printed bedgeawn then theau wore,—
    A hailstorm pattern co'ed,
Wi' linsey skirt, an' apron white,
    An' bonnet deep an' broad.

" I used to think thy e'en wur like
    Two diamonds in a well,
To get at which, an' share their leet,
    I'd tumble in mysel'.

" For weeks an' months I hung abeaut,
    An' thro yo'r window peeped ;
An' soiked, an' longed, an' fretted sore,
    But word I never cheeped.

"Till once when primed wi' fettled ale
 I'd had at th' owd Blue Bo,
I mustered pluck for t' knock at th' dur,
 An shout thy name an' o.

"My heart did pant, my yure stood up,
 But ne'er a foot I yerd,
Till th' window rickled up aboon,
 An' th' chamber curtains stirred.

"Then summat coome—piash on my yead,—
 (It wur th' neet o' th' weshin-day),
An' I fund I 're covered o'er wi' suds,
 As white as blossomed spray.

"Wi' pluck quite cooled, I crept to'ard whoam,
 But vowed within mysel',
If e'er I geet a chance to do't,
 I'd pick thee into th' well

"My mother sauced me—well hoo mit
 An' said, 'Th' dules i'th' men !
I sarved thy feyther wur than that,
 But still he coome again.

"' I'stead o' carryin' on that way,
 An' snurchin' till theau'rt blynt,
Go thee once moore an' punce at th' dur,
 An' whistle while theau's wynt.

"'An' if hoo doesno' come for that,
 There's lots on Bowman's Lea
As farrantly an' good as hoo,
 Ut would be preawd o' thee.'

" I mustered up my pluck once more
   This time beaut fettled ale—
An' swung my clogs to Katty Green,
   An' jumped yo'r garden rail.

" Crash int' a fayberry tree I leet,
   Ut under th' window grew,
An' th' noise it made thy shuttle stopt,
   An' caut thy candle blew.

" Then someb'dy come—'twur thee, owd lass !—
   I knew by th' shoinin' strip
O' leet ut shot deawn th' garden fowt ;
   An' my heart wur at my lip.

" 'Art hurt ?' theau axt. ' I am,' I said ;
   ' But th' pain I have 's inside :
No fayberry tree nor garden rail
   Had caused it if they'd tried.

" ' It's thy two een han shot me through,
   Wi' bullets made o' flame ;
An' if I dee, they'n say abeaut
   There's nobbut thee to blame.'

" ' I shouldno' like t' be hanged,' theau said,
   An' raised me to my feet ;
' So if a word 'll cure thy pain,
   I'll give it thee to-neet.'

" ' Theau said that word ; 'twur one as sweet
   As ever music trilled ;
To yer it hauve as sweet again
   I'd ten times o'er be killed.

" We made it up that neet, owd lass
    An' pledged caur love i'th poorch ;
An' when that tree bore fruit again
    We'd said ' *I will* '—at th' church. '

' Twas on their fiftieth wedding-day
    That thus old Johnny spoke ;
Nor e'er a pair on Bowman's Lea
    Had borne so light a yoke.

Their children, four, had wed away,
    And left the couple lone,
Save with the dear companionship
    Of memories sweetly known.

That day came round again, as 'twill
    When time flies quickly o'er,
And found old Johnny and his wife
    Discoursing as before.

" By th' mon ! " said he, and up he sprang,
    " I feel as young as then !
Let's fancy we'n ne'er lived this time,
    An' cooart it o'er again.

" I'll goo cautside, an' knock at th' dur,
    An' whistle—'tisno' late—
An' 'stead o' breakin' fayberry trees,
    I'll rickle th' garden gate.

" Then theau mun come, an' say to me
    That word theau said before,
An' seeal caur love i'th' poorch, as then,
    Wi' hearty smacks a score."

" Well, well," said peggy, " go thee eaut,
  An' play thy part as t' con ;
An' I'll play mine as if I'd ne'er
  Yet spokken to a mon."

Agreed,—they each their several parts
  Proceeded to fulfil ;
The old man shooked the garden gate,
  And whistled loud and shrill.

Up went the window overhead,
  The curtains fluttered white,
Then down on Johnny's hatless pate
  A shower-bath did alight.

" 'Od sink thee, Peg !" the old man cried,
  " I bargained noane for that,
Theau's weet me through ; an' did ta know
  I're here witheaut my hat ?"

" Theau's played thy part, an' I've played mine,"
  Said Peggy from her room ;
" *I've nobbut sarved thee th' same to-neet
  As I did th' fust neet theau coome.*"

A COT O' YO'R OWN.

MUSIC BY JAS. BATCHELDER.

(From " Beginning the World.")

COME, lads, lend yo'r ears, an' I'll sing you a song
  That isno' o' battle an' strife,
But peace an' good will between mon an' his kind,—
  A bond between husband an' wife.
It's be yo'r own mester an' landlord beside,
  Feight shy o' bumbailiff an' dun ;
Plant yo'r vine an' yo'r figtree afore it's too late,
  An' live in a cot o' yo'r own.

CHORUS.
  Then live for to-morn, lads, an' dunno be foos,
    But wortch an' lay by while yo' con ;
      While yo'r lithsome an' limber
      Pile up bricks an' timber,
  An' live in a cot o' yo'r own.

A mon ut's a shop-book 'll never get on,
  If he's credit he pays for't, that's sure :
Let him pay ready brass, spend no moore than he gets,
  An' he'll never be hampered nor poor.
A rent-day's a care-day as oft as it comes,
  When a londlord's as hard as a stone ;
But this weekly vexation ne'er troubles the heart
  Of a mon that's a cot of his own.
                    Then live for to-morn, &c.

Ther's one o' my neighbours, how wealthy he's grown
   Wi' lendin', and screwin', an' jobs;
But if nobody'd borrowed, an' paid double back,
   How mich better for other folk's fobs !
What yo' pay'n through yo'r nose i' both shopscores
     an' rent,
   An' interest to popshop an' "loan,"
Would soon lay th' foundations o' prosperous days,
   An' build yo' a cot o' yo'r own.
              Then live for to-morn, &c.

Yo' conno raise hay if yo' sown nowt but wynt;
   Loud talkin' 'll gather no corn ;
But delve, plough, an' harrow, an' scatter good seed,
   An' yo'n fill both yo'r meal-poke an' churn.
Then here's to a mon ut'll strive for the best,
   And lay up for owd age while he con,
An' ut ne'er shuts his dur on a shelterless friend,
   While he lives in a cot o' his own.
              Then live for to-morn, &c.

GO TAK' THE RAGGED CHILDER
AN' FLIT.

THE REVERSE SIDE OF THE PICTURE TO "COME WHOAM
TO THI CHILDREN AN' ME."

HAS caur Jammy been *here* to-neet ?
  O theau'rt *theer*, theau great dhrunken
    slotch !
It's sthrange if aw nowt elze to do
  Bo ha' thee every bed-time to fotch.
Come whoam ; or aw'll goo an' go t' bed,
  An' leeov thee t' sleep where theau art ;
For theau'rt here every neet o' thi life,
  As soon's theau gets th' hoss eaut o'th' cart.

What is ther' for th' supper ?   Ther's nowt !
  Beaut theau tak's a red herrin' fro' Sol's.
Heaw con t' think aw con get thi owt good,
  When theau leeovs me nowt bo th' bare walls ?
If theau'd gie me thi wage as theau owt,
  Aw could do summat farrantly then ;
Bo aw getten a thowt i' mi yed
  We mun ne'er ha' nowt gradely ogen.

Have aw browt thi top-cwot ?   Go thi look !
   Aw'd ha' browt thi th' *stret-jacket* as soon ;
Theau knows aw've ha' t' *qut it up th' speaut*,
   For money to pay for thi shoon.
Ther's rent-chap just bin, an' he swears
   He can never catch nob'dy a-whoam :
He's bin four or five times to-day,
   Bo aw'r *caut*, an' aw couldna weel come.

Nawe ; I ha'na bin dhrinkin' misel ;
   Aw've ne'er tastut "tiger " to-day ;
Bo aw bin o'er to Plattin' to yo'r Nan's,
   An' hoo would mak' mi t' stop to mi tae.
If we han had a toothful o' rum,
   Hoo paid for 't, an' that's nowt to thee :
If it's done me some good, *thee* ne'er fret—
   Bo theau never thinks nowt about *me*.

What's made thee bring th' childher yon toys?
   Theau't likker t' ha' browt thi brass whoam ;
For Sal has poo'd th' yead off her doll,
   An' Dick's sent his clog through his dhrum ;
An' then ther's yon fal-dher-dal cap,
   Stick't full o' pink ribbons, theau's browt ;
If theau'd browt mi two black uns i'th' stid,
   Theau'd ha' done summat like as theau owt.

Will t' come whoam ?   Then tarry wheer t' art
   For aw'm cussed if aw ax thee ogen ;
Eh ! this world 'ud soon be at an eend
   If wimmen wur owt like yo' men.

Nawe! aw'll see thi befar 'fore aw'll sup,
　　Aw'd reyther throw th' pot at thi yead ;
An aw've twenty good minds for to do't,
　　If it's nobbut for what theau's just sed.

Will t' hit mi?　Ay, do, if theau dar !
　　An' aw'll just ha' thi walkt eaut o'th' dur ;
Theau thinks, 'cose theau plaguet *t'other wife*,
　　Theau'll ha *me* at th' same rate as theau'd *her*
Bo aw'll show thi a sperrit, mi lad,
　　'At'll noa tak' a blow for a buss ;
An' if t' tries thi owd capers wi' me,
　　As bad as theau does aw'll do wus.

So wind up thi lip an' chew that,
　　An' tarry o neet if theau will ;
If they'n tak thi, an' keep thi, it's reet,
　　For aw'm blest if aw've not had mi fill.
If theaurt toyart o' livin wi' me,—
　　Go, tak' thi ragged childher an' flit,
For if t' byets me to th' seet o' mysel',
　　Theau'll ne'er mak' mi t' cruttle a bit.

BILL BABBY'S FROLIC.

A FAILSWORTH STORY OF PETERLOO.

BILL Babby went to Peterloo,
  By patriotism or fancy led ;
But what's more likely, love of fun,
  Or ought that tumbled int' his yead.

He'd seen that morn a mug o' stew,
  Just flakin' o'er wi' fat i'th' oon,
Wi' marjoram, an' other yarbs,
  To mak it sweet—rare wark for th' spoon.

Ther howsome "slip-throat" hung i' rags,
  An' sweet oatcakes, just nicely browned
I'th' front o'th' fire—made clogs feel leet—
  They bounced like corks when touchin' th' ground.

Bill geet a carter's dose o' this,
  Then of he went to Peterloo ;
He'd fotch the dule fro' eaut his den,
  When backed wi' some three pints o' stew.

So grand a day he had not seen—
  So mony lasses donned i' white !
Wi' banners wavin—what a seet !—
  To mak his heart jump wi' delight.

But th' fun were o'er ere it began—
  Bill knew, by th'sound, ther summat wrong ;
But what it wur he could no' tell
  That moved an' swelled that mighty throng.

He thowt tw'ur time t' be leeavin th' row
  To those ut like't to feight it eaut,
But when he tried to stir— by th' mass !
  He fund no road to get abeaut.

At last he spied a narrow gate
  That led to streets unknown before ;
An' feeling safe fro' cut-throat harm,
  He whistled, sang, an' sometimes swore.

Whene'er he yerd the sound o' strife
  Come nearer, he backed int' his hole,
Where he stood peepin' like a rat,
  But venture out !—not for his soul.

There coome a wind-fall straight fro' th' clouds,
  A new French horn, o' glittering brass,
Lay like a tempting bit o' gowd,
  Or honest smile fro' winsome lass.

Bill blew a blast on that theere horn
  That sounded like the crack o' doom,
Or jackass wi' its tail teed down,
  Or wayver gruntin' at his loom.

Just then a troop o' horsemen rode
　　Reet past wheere Bill had pitched his tent,
Or rayther wheere he'd crommed his rags—
　　Then th' second blast the welkin rent.

The horsemen reeled—the horses' hoofs
　　Struck fire as back the heroes rode ;
Bill blew an' blew till th' troopers swore
　　They'rn no far off th' dule's abode.

Soon th' street wur cleared, then out Bill crept,
　　An' fund he'd Newton Lone t' hissel ;
An', when he'd seeted th' " pow," he said
　　T'wur th' fust time e'er he'd bin i' h——

MORAL.

Whene'er yor on a frolic bent,
　　Don't go to scenes like Peterloo ;
Nor blow a horn i' th' d——l's band
　　Unless yor poke's well lined wi' *stew*.

THE GARDENER AND HIS FLOWERS.

WHY do I dwell alone, you ask,
    With ne'er a soul my lot to share?
These children have such claims on me
    That I have little love to spare.

My children? Yes, I mean my flowers;
    They prattle to me just like bairns,
They speak a language of their own,
    Which only a loving parent learns.

They're at their morning prayers now;
    You'll see them fold their tiny hands,
To lisp their orisons like babes,
    Obedient to God's commands.

You'll see them look at me, and smile,
    As 'tis their wont when prayers are said;
They're not like children of the poor,
    Who have to earn their daily bread.

They toil not, neither do they spin,
    When on the Mount, our Saviour said,
Yet Solomon, with all his pride,
    Was not like one of these arrayed.

They give me no anxieties
    About their hats, and shoes, and socks ;
Nor ought they wear.   They're quite content
    To cloth their limbs with robes or frocks.

From these, the meek-eyed monitors,
    Our maidens might a lesson take ;
They show no airs, put on no " side,"
    As if God's work they would unmake.

They're quite contented with their lot,
    Nor care if riches came in showers ;
If they bedeck the paths of queens,
    They won't forget they're only flowers.

It grieves me when they're short of rain,
    With not a drop to wet their lips ;
But, oh, how thankful each one seems,
    When dew, like liquid gems, it sips.

I'm fretful only when one dies,
    To see it droop its tiny head,
And smile a farewell to the sun ;
    Ah, then I know the flower is dead !

THOU'RT LONELY, MY JAMMIE.

THOU'RT lonely, my Jammie, art ill, or i' love ?
  Thou goes mopsin, an' sighin' about ;
An' thy clooas don't fit thee as weel as they did—
  Thou'rt like a poor leet goin' out.
Han they vexed thee, or what maks thy lip hang so low?
  Or hast' lost o thy marbles again ?
But they sigh noane o'er marbles, nor fret when they're
    lost—
  Thou'rt i' *love* ; that to me is quite plain.

Thou'rt quick goin' out, but thou'rt slow momin' in,
  An' thy clogs seem too big for thy feet ;
They're too heavy to trail when thou'rt gooin' t' thy
    wark,
  But leetsome an' limber at neet.
An' thy nose aulus points to'ard Owd Johnny Brookes'
    farm,
  As if pigeons wur flyin' o'er th' roof ;
But I think Johnny's lass has moore likins to thee,
  At neet, when hoo's trippin deawn th' cloof.

Thou'rt moane like thy feyther when he coome to me,
  He did no' stond starin' at nowt,
He'd ha' stood at th' heause-end, an' ha' whistled an'
    sung,
  Till thy gronfeyther'd ha' punsed him deawn th' fowt.
Then ha' shown up th' neet after as brazent as brass,
  An' into eaur heause chuckt his hat,
Neaw, Jammie, if t' wants to get th' heart of a lass,
  Show some pluck, an' hoo'll like thee for that.

Neaw go thy ways off, lad, an' come noane again,
    Till wi' Jennie theau's made it o reet.
I know ut th' lass likes thee, but connot for shame
    To ax thee t' walk eaut of a neet.
Owd Johnnie 'll no' like it when he gets to know ;
    He thinks daisies an' mayfleawers o' Jane.
He'll grumble an' swear, but he'll hardly say " No,"
    When he comes to his senses again.

Jammie's off like a greyhound ut's just seen a hare,
    An' what time he'll come back nob'dy knows.
If he's gone i' good yearnest I dunno' mich care,
    Lest owd Johnnie an' he come to blows.
Eh, this coortin's rough wark, but I'd rayther 'twur so,
    Than this makkin th' heause nice for him t' come,
There's honester sweethearts stond whistlin' at th' dur,
    Than are welcomed as if they'rn awhoam.

It's reet !   There's eaur Jammie, I know by his foot ;
    Catch a mother not knowin' by th' seaund.
An' he's managed his job ; summat towd me he'd dot't,
    An' we're gladsome an' happy o reaund.
Come, Jammie, an' buss thy owd mother i'th' nook,
    There's nowt like a good, honest face ;
I knew if theau gan th' lass a fair lovin' look,
    In her heart, lad, hoo'd find thee a place.

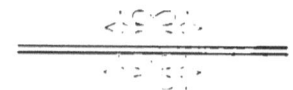

LITTLE ANNIE'S BIRDS.

A LESSON OF KINDNESS.

THE snow lay on the ground, and made
　　A Druid of each oak,
When Annie stepped from the kitchen door
　　To feed her feathered folk.

They flew in circlets round, and perched
　　In chattering groups about ;
Some fanned the snow from clothes-line stumps,
　　And others shared a spout.

Then down they came in quick descent,
　　Soon as the crumbs were spread ;
And Annie's glee shone out in smiles
　　At each waggling tail and head.

She knows which are the baby birds—
　　They are so wild at first, and shy ;
But as they grow they get more bold,
　　And push their elders by.

"'Tis naughty of them," she admits,
　　"And selfish, too," she says ;
"But who can blame them for it, when
　　So *human* are their ways ?"

She loved to see upon the snow
　　The prints of tiny feet,
Like patterns traced on summer dews,
　　Where fairies nightly meet.

" You won't come when the snow is gone,
　And summer brings you food,
To pick the seeds, and flowers, and fruit,
　To feed your little brood ? "

Thus Annie spoke, and round there went
　A twittering that said " No ;"
And Annie gave her word that she
　Would feed them during snow

The pledge was kept ; each summer time,
　When gardens suffered most,
Of Annie's little crop of peas
　Not one was to her lost.

The birds would come and sing for her,
　Or chatter from each tree,
But ne'er descend to garden bed,
　Or with the fruit make free.

Thus kindness an immunity
　From pilf'ring had secured,
And neighbours wondered at the cause,
　Whilst they such thefts endured.

Ah me ! my friends, when you are bent
　On strife-begetting words,
Take council, and a lesson learn
　From Annie and her birds.

THE CAMBRIAN'S WELCOME TO THE QUEEN,

ON HER MAJESTY'S VISIT TO NORTH WALES, AUGUST, 1889.

HAIL, chief of England's royal race!
    The sons of Cambria welcome thee;
But not with conquered spirit bowed,
    Nor hearts bereft of chivalry.

The hands that once in mailéd might,
    The foeman seized with deadly grasp,
And wielded battle-axe and sword,
    Now folded are in friendly clasp.

Dead are the feuds of bygone years;
    And buried 'neath embattled towers;
And where the blood of Kings hath flowed,
    Is now bedight with Peace's flowers.

Thou'rt welcome to this glorious land,
    Where for their homes the Cymri fought;
And love of freedom nerved the arm
    That erst great deeds of valour wrought.

Who would not fight for land so fair,
    Each mountain, stream, and forest green,
Where Nature in her grandeur sits—
    A crownless—not a throneless Queen?

G

Each mountain is a regal throne;
    Each stream a harp whose echoes raise
The tones that thrill the Cambrian's breast
    With memories of warlike days.

But rings not now the clarion's note,
    That summoned to the field of strife,
When Celt and Saxon met in fray,
    And gave to slaughter life for life.

Thou hear'st the roll of other sounds,
    The hymn of praise bestowed on thee,
By children of thine ancient foes,
    And tuned to " bardic " minstrelsy;

The strange, weird music of the past,
    That fills us with religious awe,
And bends the knee to worship forms
    Whereon is writ Creation's law.

We pray thee not forget this day,
    When homed within thy Saxon hall;
But think what love thy presence wakes,
    When patriotism and duty call.

Visiting at Llangollen,
    August 26th, 1889.

TO HENRY IRVING, ESQ.,

PRESIDENT OF "THE ARTS CLUB," MANCHESTER.

FRIEND Irving, let me shake thy neive,
    If but in spirit. I would weave
A song to thee; but that I'll leave
            To abler pens,—
But not more honest, I believe,
            Than poor old Ben's.

Thou hast essayed the highest rung
Of Fame's steep ladder. Pen and tongue
Have each thy well-earned praises sung
            In tuneful strain;
And e'en thy pæans have been rung
            Across the main.

Thou'lt know me? The old "Titan Club,"
With name Shakespearian* did me dub.
It was not "Hamlet,"—"There's the rub,"—
            But now I've got em,—
May every Thespian set his tub
            On its own "Bottom!"

   *Every member of the Titan Club had to assume the name of one
of Shakespear's characters. The writer's name was "Bottom,"
the Weaver.

I trust that on Life's busy stage
I've played a part—from youth to age;
Nor shrank from ought that did engage
                    My humble wits;
But eyed with fear the critic's page,
                    And where he sits.

I've played at times in many parts;
But never dealt in broken hearts,
Nor meddled much with Cupid's darts,—
                    (I've shot a true one.)
When from his line a fool departs,
                    He's something t' rue on.

I've done my shout among the rabble,
And easy "lengths" have dared to babble;
I've played a "king," but failed grab all
                    His royal treasure.
In poetry I've dared to dabble,
                    Just for my pleasure.

How many messages I've borne
To dukes and lords and braved their scorn!—
Which messages were often torn,
                    Or trod to dust,
Because the vintner said he'd sworn
                    No further trust.

As "Seacoal" I got taunts and blows,
Because the pimple on my nose
(Quite big enough for bud of rose)
                    Had made me squint.
George Sheffield put on't all the glows
                    Of "Bardolph's" tint.

Melpomene, the peevish slut,
Persuaded me I need but strut
And shout " The time *will* come !" to put
                    Cash in thy purse,
But found by practising I got
                    From bad to worse.

Now I'm a long way past my noon,
And in the "slippered pantaloon,"
The last age I shall be in soon,
                    Whate'er 'twill bring
Sans eyes ; sans teeth (fed with a spoon) :
                    Sans everything.

THE FAIR DRUMMER BOY.

" I'M off to the wars, love, to fight for Old England ;
  Oh weep not, dear Mary, that now we must part ;
Though torn from thy presence to cross the wide billow,
  Thine image shall leave not this fond loving heart. "

Thus spoke a brave guardsman, his foot on the gangway ;
  The sails of the transport unfurled to the wind.
It was not faint heart wrung the sigh from his bosom ;
  But leaving his Albion and Mary behind.

Up went the anchor, away sped each vessel
  That bore a brave army to Spain's rocky coast ;
And soon in the smoke and the tumult of battle,
  The image of love to our hero was lost

One night, as he lay by the camp-fire reposing,
  A sweet, gentle voice whispered thus in his ear :
" Oh let not the sigh break thy wound-soothing slumber,
  But rest, dearest rest, for thy Mary is near."

He starts!   Hark! the trumpet to battle is calling;
  The drum rolls its thunder; the sword flashes bare;
Up, up, ye brave guardsmen, the eagle is screeching,
  And flapping its wings in the dull morning air!

The sun gazed once more on that field red with carnage;
  The dead and the dying lay thick on the ground;
When a *drummer boy* knelt by a wounded young guards-
    man,
  And whisper'd of *love* while he bound up the wound.

"Who art thou, my youngster, that com'st with such
    tidings,
  To cheer me in sorrow?" the soldier he cried;
But the boy answer'd not, for a stray shot came flying,
  And *Mary* fell dead by her true lover's side.

WHOAM-BREWED.

(From " Irkdale," &c.)

THER'S nowt i' this wo'ld like my own chimdy nook,
  When my cheear up to th' fire I've poo'd ;
When th' wife has just rocked th' little babby to sleep,
  An' fotched me a mug o' whoam-brewed.

Hoo smiles, does th' owd dame, as if nobbut just wed,
  When her caps an' her napkins hoo's blued,
Then warms up her face wi' a blink o' th' owd leet
  Ut shines in a mug o' whoam-brewed.

It's as breet as a glent o' caur Maytime o' life,
  Or as havin' owd pleasures renewed,
Is the sunleet ut fo's reaund my hearthstone at neet,
  When seen through a sheawer o' whoam-brewed.

My heause is my castle has often bin sung,
  Where no king, duke, or lord dar' intrude ;
But it needs no hard feightin to keep eaut a foe
  When I truce wi' a mug o' whoam-brewed.   .

Care once coome a-neighbourin', an' pottert at th' dur
  An' his nose into th' keyhole he screwed ;
But he soon scampered back to his feyther, the dule,
  When he smelt I'd a mug o' whoam-brewed.

When I'm thinkin' what toilin' an' frabbin' ther` needs
  Through this wo'ld to get decently poo'd,
It melts into pastime, does th' hardest o' wark,
  When it's helped wi' a mug o' whoam-brewed.

It'll help us to fettle both th' nation an' th' laws,
  An' to so'der up mony a feud ;
An' if th' wo'ld has gone wrang, we con reet it again
  By th' power of a mug o' whoam-brewed.

Then come to my elbow, thou primest o' drinks,
  Wi' sweetest o' pleasures endued ;
The jolliest neighbour to jog wi' through life
  Is a full peauchin mug o' whoam-brewed.

TH' OWD TIN KETTLE.

I'M a merry little kettle,
　　For I sing when I'm i' fettle ;
Besides that, I can tell a good tale.
　　I spit, and I sputter,
　　Like a tooad in a gutter,
When they fill my old belly wi' brown ale ;
　　I'd rayther it wur wayter,
　　For a drop o' the "crayter,"
Or an owd-fashint baggin—tae and rum.
　　Then th' steeam fro' my spout
　　Maks th' childer give a shout,
An' they makken th' kitchen table int' a drum.

　　They wanten me for th' tae,
　　Whether hyson or Bohay,
(There's noather on 'em good until they're brewed)
　　An' I give th' owd mon a wink,
　　When he's sittin' deawn to drink,
Tae that's fit for nowt but th' pigs, becose it's stewed.

But merrily I sing
When o' beauty there's a ring
Round the table, an' the toast is smokin' hot ;
Then loud is the chatter,
As the cups an' saucers clatter,
An' th' ambrosia goes ploppin out o' th' pot.

To the music of the mill
Grindin' coffee, I am still ;
I like to hear the sound when it's in tune.
Then th' aroma from the pot,
When my water's bilin' hot,
Is like turnin' frosty Kesmus into June.
Who wouldno' be a kettle
If they're made o' th' sort o' metal
Ut'll polish like a shillin' when it's new ?
When th' hearthstone's warm an' breet,
And young folk sit round at neet,
Oh, of merrier little kettles there are few !

AB-O'TH'-YATE'S WELCOME TO PRINCE ALBERT VICTOR,

ON HIS VISIT TO MANCHESTER, OCTOBER 27TH, 1888.

(With an apology to Edwin Waugh.)

COME, Sarah, get thy bonnet on,
　An' gang along wi' me,
An' we'n go deawn to Manchester,
　This royal lad to see.
They say'n his face is like his mam's,
　His e'en are like his dad's ;
But i' other things, if th' truth wur known,
　He's mich like other lads.

His pasture's bin too rich for him—
　He seldom porritch takes ;
An' nobd'y'll e'er be plagued wi' fat
　That feeds on Eccles cakes.
If he'll come deawn to Daisy Nook,
　Wi' Charlie, Frank, an' me,
We'n show him heaw to ratch his rags
　Wi' a cheese an' bacon spree.

We'n taich him heaw to swing his clogs,
  An' heaw to use his spoon ;
An' heaw to whet an appetite
  By peepin' into th' oon—
An' seein' theere a bubblin' tin,
  Just like a little sac ;
An' I'll be sworn when he goes whoam
  He'll want no moore tae.

We'n pile some flesh on his bare bones,
  Ut are grinnin' through his skin,
An' mak' him he'll no' know hissel
  Before a week he's bin.
An' when wi' th' " Hencote's " fun an' song,
  He's yerd the rafters ring,
He'll say—" Sup up, lads, I'll stond th' next—
  I'm ' every inch a king ! '"*

* " Ay, every inch a King."—*King Lear.*

GYPSIES.

THRO' Cheetham Hill one summer day
   I took a leisure tramp,
When down beside the Irk I came
   Upon a gypsies' camp.

I knew they were gypsies by the roof
   Of each wain-top shaped tent,
And canvas walls supported by
   Strong ribs of ash-tree, bent.

The gate being open, in I went,
   And scared the ducks and hens
That quacked and chucked behind the bars
   And nets of several pens.

The " king " stood by in robe of state
   (A jacket brown and patched),
And when I hailed his majesty,
   His royal head he scratched.

" Do these perch out of doors ? " I ask,
   As down the food he chucks;
He shrugs his shoulders, then replies—
   " The hens do—not the ducks. "

I knew by that I'd met a wag,
  Albeit a gypsy chief;
And none would have suspected him
  Of being a poultry thief.

We talked of breeding—eggs, and chicks,
  And pullets by the way;
But whether breeding paid or not,
  The " king " had nought to say.

" I've tried to hatch some chicks, " he said,
  " But the deuce was in my luck ;
They pined and died.   What was the cause ?
  The beggars wouldn't *suck*. "

I tried him on another tack—
  This time to excite his fear—
" Arn't you afraid of *thieves* ? " I asked,
  " Or hen-roost 'cracks' being near ?

I saw he knew my meaning by
  The way he threw his smiles—
" *The ain't a gypsy Camp*." said he,
  " *But this within ten miles*."

" WE ARE ON OUR JOURNEY HOME."

THE church-bells rang with a cheerful chime,
  And the sun was sinking low,
As tired with play the children tramped,
  With weary steps and slow.
They were overcome by their holiday jaunt,
  And no farther cared to roam ;
But they sang as with a joyful heart,
  " We are on our journey home."

The children cheered as the milk-pails clang
  Their thirsty gathering hailed,
And buns were flying like balls at play,
  And the baskets never failed.
The birds were watching the children feed,
  Expecting that their turn would come ;
Then the children sang as a parting song—
  " We are on our journey home."

An old man bent 'neath a load of years,
  His partner by his side,
Was gazing upward with vision dim
  At a sign on a post, then sighed.
" We are on the right road, love," the old man said,
  When he'd read this wooden tome ;
" 'This way to the workhouse'—come darling bear
    up,
  We are on our journey home.

"Nay, turn not to look," the old man said,
    "It is not the church on the hill,
Where our dear one lies; we could look on her
        grave,
    When we lived in the cot by the mill.
They are not the old bells we have list to so oft,
    In the grey of the evening's gloam,
That seemed to say with a mournful voice,
    ' You are on your journey home.' "

"Ah never more shall we hear those bells,
    Nor look on the dear one's bed,
Nor trim the flowers that grow at their feet,
    And garland her flaxen head.
I care not how short this journey will be,
    Nor how soon the time may come,
When the kindly earth will be soft to our feet,
    And we've ended our journey home."

Then towards the workhouse they wandered on,
    But gave a farewell sigh,
When they'd looked their last on the cot they'd left,
    And the graves where their kindred lie.
They are resting now from their earthly task;
    No more from their dwelling they'll roam,
In heaven they've found eternal repose;
    They have finished their journey home.

H

HARD TIMES.

(SONG.)

"YO' may talk o' hard times," said old Abram o'
        Dan's,
"But yo'n nobbut touched th' fringe on 'em yet.
They'rn harder when bacon wi' th' scithors wur cut,
    An' porritch no wayver could get ;
When th' wynt would blow through yo' as if you'rn a
        sieve,
    An' whistled the keener it froze :
When we'd nothin' to fence cawr cowd bodies 'gen th'
        cowd,
    But creep-o'ers, an' howd-teh-bi-th'-wohs.*

"They'n hard times when a crust o' Breawn George wur
        too hard
    For rottans to drag i' their holes ;
When childer wur more scientific than rats,
    And bor'd for 't, like borin' for coals.
They made a big hole i' th' timbers o'er th' shelf,
    Heaw they're done it, wheay, nobody knows :
But th' crust o' Breawn George disappeared like a ghost,
    Then 'twur creep-o'ers, an' howd-teh-bi-th'-wohs.

" It wur dangerous t' turn eawt wi' yo'r owler new
    greased,
For yo'rn sure to be tackled by dogs.
If they'd smelt mutton fat they'd ha set yo' i' th' lone,
    An' etten both tops off yo'r clogs.
If a bakin'-day happened, though seldom one coome,
    My feyther'd get ready for blows ;
He'd ha guarded th' oon dur like sentry i' th' wars,
    More creep-o'ers, an' howd-teh-bi-th'-wohs.

No pawnbroker strove eaut o' th' custom he geet,
    Becose folk had nothin' to pop ;
They'd takken their rags till they'd none they could
    spare,
    Unless they'd ha' striped 'em i' th' shop.
Little help could be squeezed eaut o' th' rich i' thoose
    days,
    Noather i' mayte, fire, nor " thank yo, sir " clothes ;
They walled reaund their heauses, an' shut up their
    hearts,
    When we'd creep-o'ers an' howd-teh-bi-th'-wohs.

" I've worn eaut my owler i' lookin' for wark,
    But of wark thore wur none to be had ;
When th' mice emigrated, an' deed upo' th' road,
    An' wi' th' rottans—why, things wur as bad.
When th' brids coome i' flocks to a cottager's dur,
    An' showed 'em their frost-bitten toes ;
An' heaw slackly their feathers hung on to their backs,
    They couldno' ate howd-teh-bi th'-wohs.

I think it quite time these owd limbs wur at rest,
  Or on their long journey to'ard whoam,
Wheere there's no frost or snow, an' no yammerin'
      hearts
  Nor hauve naked bodies con come.
I yerd a voice saying, " Ye sufferers on earth,
  Come hither and try your new clothes !
For the poor shall be rich, and the rich all alike—
  No moore creep-o'ers or howd-teh-bi-th'-wohs."

---

* *Creep-o'ers*—" Creep over Stiles." *Howd teh-bi-th'-wohs*—" Howd-
thee-by-the-walls," a kind of gruel sweetened with treacle.   See
" Tum Grunt and Whistle Pig," by K. Walker.

THE BEAUTIFUL SNOW.

A PARODY.

OH, the beautiful snow! The beautiful snow,
How gently it falls on the earth below,
Like fleece newly blown from Ganymede's crest,
And floating away to some airy nest.

Says Johnny-i'-th'-Nook, "Come eaut an' slur,"
Then fo's on his back at his gronfeyther's dur;
"Oh, that wur a bang!" he shouted. "Oh, oh!"
The beautiful, beautiful, beautiful snow!

Oh, the beautiful snow, the beautiful snow!
See it whirl through the air as the rude wind blows;
Now weaves it a web of its gossamer flakes,
As along the valley it's course it takes.

Says Betty-at-Robin's, "Eh, what a nice slide!
As breet as a kettle—I'll just have a ride;
Come, stick to my hont!!!—why didta let go?"
The beautiful, beautiful, beautiful snow!

Oh, the beautiful snow, the beautiful snow!
Now sweeps o'er the moor like a merciless foe,
And creeps under doors like a cowardly elf,
Afraid of the storm it created itself.

Owd Matty-o'-Besom's has gone eaut o'th' heause,
An' made to'ard a slide, as quiet as a meause;
"I'll give it yond madam!" but strikes not a blow—
Hoo's measurt her length on the beautiful snow.

SAM BAMFORD'S GRAVE.

A CHRISTMAS IDYL.

I STOOD beside Sam Bamford's grave,
  Ut looks o'er Middle-teawn,
An' th' owd lad woke within his yearth,
  An' said, " Wheere arta beaun ? "

' I'm gooin' deawn to Shuttlewo'th's
  At th' sign o'th' Owd Boar's Yead,
To meet a ' Raker ' friend or two,
  An' have a gill," I said.†

" Wheay, wheay, what's up, like ? Is it th'
    Wakes ?
  Or is it th' Show ? " said Sam.
" I fain would like t' goo wi' thee, lad ;
  It's dryish wheere I am.

" Is Ned wi' thee, or Page or Jim ?
  Is Joe or Charley theere ?
'Lijah's gone whoam, I know, poor lad !
  He'd little t' stop for here.

† See " Tim Bobbin's Grave," by Sam Bamford.

"Come, tell me o' an' moore beside,
   I'm 'hutchin fain' to yer it ;
There's nob'dy coes to tell me owt,
   Nobbut neaw an' then a sperrit,

" Ut's bin a-makkin' furnityer
   To caper on some floor.
Han poets begun a-bankin' yet ?
   Are publishers come poor ?

" Han Frenchmen ta'en to scaur kreaut ?
   Is Livingston come whoam ?
Are pa'sons gan o'r fratchin' yet ?
   Is th' Church gone o'er to Rome ?

" Are th' Yankees talkin' leaud an' tall ?
   Is Ireland satisfied ?
Han' th' Garmons drawn their feightin' brass ?
   Has th' ballot e'er bin tried ?

" Are skoo-boards happy families ?
   Does eddication thrive ?
Is charity owt but a name ?
   Is *self*-ism still alive ?

" What is it's browt thee here to-dey ?
   Hast' bizness wi' the d'yed ?
Or arta come'n a trimmin' th' fleawers
   That hem eaur little bed ?"

" I've come to chose a spot on which
   To raise a stone," I said.
" Thy native teawn con gie thee *that*,
   If it couldno' find thee bread."

" What, what," he said—" a moniment !—
    A moniment to *me* ?
Just lift that quarried keaunterpane,
    An' help to set me free.

" I'll moniment 'em—that I will—
    A changeful, wayward crew !
Fust backbite me, then co me spy,
    An' th' Judas o' Peterloo !

" *They* raise a moniment to *me* !
    Believe in no sich thing ;
They'd rayther have a jumpin' match,
    Or creawn a sond-chap king.

" I need no moniment—not I ;
    Well, not o' sculptured stone.
Look i' my ' Radical '—it's theere—
    A tablet o' my own.

" Good deeds are their own moniments,
    A biggish mon hath said ;
Good lives leave tracks that th' feet o' time
    Pass o'er wi' kindly tread.

" Gi'e bread to th' poor, to th' weak give help,
    Mak' hearthstones warm an' breet ;
A lesson taich to th' rich an' preaud,
    To darkened minds give leet.

" An' if, when yo'n this duty done,
    Yo'n gether reawnd my grave,
An' sing a hymn o' thankful praise,
    I'll help yo' wi' a stave.

" Neaw goo an' tell 'em what I've said ;
   But if they're bent on stone,
Wheay, let 'em set abeaut it, then,
   An' mak' their purpose known.

" An' let not year on year go past,
   An' Wakes an' Show get o'er,
Then find theirsels at th' end o' time
   Just wheere they wur before.

" If *we'd* stood still i' thoose dark days
   When patriots pined an' bled,
Heaw would yo'r minds have neaw been stored,
   Yo'r bodies clothed an' fed ?

" Where would yo'r Lancashire ha' bin,
   O' which yo'r o so preaud ?
Yo'r forges and yo'r factories
   That now its valleys creawd !

" But I'm happen a bit crankey, lad—
   They'n made me so wi' scorn ;
But bless 'em o ! Neaw let me sleep
   Till breaks my second morn."

Sam laid *him* deawn, an' gan a grunt,
   Said, " Mima, love, art' here ?"
An' I left him to his noble rest,
   Wi' a freshly-started tear.

P R O L O G U E.

(Intended by the author to have been delivered at the
Masonic Concert in aid of the boys' school, given at the Free
Trade Hall, but, through some misunderstanding, left out of the
programme.)

YE sons of Charity—and daughters too,
  We must not leave you out, it would not do
To treat our fair ones to so grave a slight,
Considering they're here with us to-night.
We'll call you sisters ; that will make amends
For human thoughtlessness, so let's be friends.
Time was when charity was but a name—
An empty word that added nought to fame :
Till woman ventured in that void alone,
Struck out a plan, and made the work her own ;
Sought out the needy, succoured the distressed,
And made the desert-home one truly blest.

'Twere no disgrace to aid in such a plan,
And give our sisters all the help we can ;
They're sure to help their brothers when in need,
Their presence here to-night were help indeed !
They know 'tis better than to imitate
The gilded virtues of the Roman State.
A guarded prudence can be too severe,
If down the cheek unheeded rolls the tear.

To be austerely just, and wise, and brave ;
But show no mercy to the suppliant slave,—
Begging for life that he might fill his days,
Training his children into virtue's ways.

A voice went forth ere breathed the human race,
" Let there be light," and darkness fled apace.
Then rose the fount of life, the glorious son,
At once he starts his heavenly course to run.
Ages have passed, and still that cry's the same :
" Let there be light ! " a cry without an aim.
Millions have heard it —scattered o'er the earth—
But still 'twas chaos till the voice went forth—
" Let there be intellectual light ! " Then furled
The cloud ; and Shakspere rose t' illume the world.

Thou Great Diffuser of that heavenly light
Throughout the universe, be here to-night.
And aid the work attempted in Thy name ;
To erring mortals none a nobler aim.
And, oh, Great Architect ! a Temple raise,
In which Thy worshippers may sound Thy praise ;
And fix for ever in the central porch—
To radiate o'er the world—Thy sacred torch !
Though shown in symbols, Learning is the light,
To brighten which we're gathered here to-night.
May Light and Charity the orphans bless !
To guide through life, to shelter from distress !
So now prepare we for the song and jest,
We've done our share—come, Minstrels, do the rest.

ARTHUR SULLIVAN LODGE, 2156·

RED BILL'S MONKEY.

"OWD POOT" drew up to th' fire one neet,
    An' charged his pipe wi' 'bacco ;
An' Red Bill's monkey grinned i'th' nook—
    A monkey they co'ed "Jacko."

"Ay, theau may bite thy cheean," said Poot,
    "But theau'll remember th' mortar ;
An' if theau tries to work again
    They'll mak' it a bit shorter."

"*Work*, did yo' say ? " "Ay, work," said Poot,
    " He's a janious in his way ;
He's up to owt fro' plasterin'
    To makkin a sope o' tae.

" I're daubin' up some holes one day,
    An while I swigged my porter,
He picked up th' trowel, an' catchin' th' cat,
    He filled her meauth wi' mortar.

"Another time he're watchin' Nell
    Mak' tae for a lot o' women,
An' thinkin' he could mend her work,
    He th' hearthstone set a swimmin'.

" He watched her wheere hoo th' caddie put,
  On th' chimbdy shelf o'er th' fire ;
But if hoo'd known what th' monkey meant
  Hoo'd surely ha' put it higher.

" Her back wur turned, then up went Jack,
  Ere yo' could say 'God bless all !'
Then th' box he seized, an liftin' th' lid,
He emptied th' tae i'th' ess-hole.

" Then down he coome, like Steeple Jack,
  An' jumped on th' hob to th' kettle,
An' emptied that on th' hearthstone, too,
  Thinkin' his job to settle.

" Jack thowt he could improve o' what
  A mon or wench could do,
By stoppin' holes that drank his milk,
  An, tae by whulsale brew.

"Oh, poor owd Jack, !—he'll work no moore,
  He're gettin' too fast for th' age ;
An' what wur th' use when o he geet
  Wur a cheean i'stead o' wage ? "

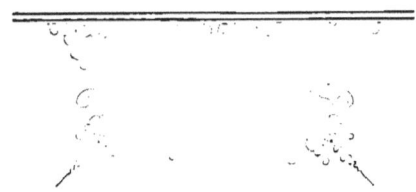

"I'RE LIVIN' WHEN BONEY* WUR TA'EN."

THERE was an old dame used to come down our
        lane,
    And at walking you'd not find her match ;
She lived all alone in a one-storey cot,
    And the roof of this dwelling was thatch.
She knew not her age any more than the clock,
    " But I're born o' Good Friday they say'n ;
" An' somewheer abeaut th' time ut th' Embargo wur
        kilt,
    " But I're livin' when Boney wur ta'en."

No bonnet she'd worn since last rushcart was made ;
    But a napkin tied o'er her cap screen
Made her face like two roses just bitten with frost,
    Leaving traces of what they had been.
" You've seen something, Betty," the neighbours
        would say,
    " Ay, moor than I want t'see again."
Then she'd shake her old head—dust her pipe on the
        bar—
    " I're livin' when Boney wur ta'en."

A widow some years old Betty had been,
    But none ever heard her repine.
" If I wanted to fish for a husband," she'd say,
    " I've nobbut to throw in my line.

---

* When the First Napoleon was taken prisoner.

" Yo young uns done nowt but keep sidlin' abeaut,
" An lookin' as if yo'rn i' pain.
" I' my day 'twur snap-an-go-bang, an' get wed—
" But I're livin' when Boney wur ta'en."

On a dark winter night an old lantern she'd swing,
  A lantern without horn or glass.
If the wind blew the light out, as oft was the case,
  She'd say, " Drat yo, lads ! let me pass."
If she'd rubbed 'gainst a stump in the darkness,
    she'd say,
  " Neaw, Jammie, theau'rt auvish, it's plain,
" But I'st ne'er end my wits wi' a monkey like thee ;
  " I're livin' when Boney wur ta'en."

For singing and dancing old Betty'd no match,
  Though only one song could she sing.
It was of one Chinaman, " Twinkle Tum Twang,"
  And the chorous was " Ding, a-ding, ding."
This song would she hum at from morning till night,
  Then up with the layrock again ;
And if her voice failed her, " Ah, well," she would say,
  " I're livin' when Boney wur ta'en "

Old Betty, with living alone, was afraid
  Lest theives might her front door assail.
So when she went shopping she took out the key,
  And hung it outside on a nail.
But poor old Betty, she could not get warm
  That winter the snow filled the lane.
Then she said, " if owd Jack comes again he may
    sit,—
  " He're livin' when Boney wur ta'en."

THE WEAVER OF WELBROOK.

(From " Chronicles of Waverlow.")

YO gentlemen o wi' yo'r hounds an' yo'r parks,
    Yo may gamble an' sport till yo' dee ;
But a quiet heause nook, a good wife, an' a book,
    Are more to the likin's o me - e.
            Wi' my pickers an' pins,
            An' my wellers to th' shins,
        My linderins, shuttle, an' yealdhook,
            My treadles an sticks,
            My weight-ropes an' bricks,—
    What a life !—said the Wayvor o' Welbrook.

I careno' for titles, nor heauses, nor lond,
    Owd Jone's a name fittin' for me ;
An' gie me a thatch, wi' a wooden-dur latch,
    An' six feet o' greaund when I dee - e.
                          Wi' my pickers, &c.

Some folk liken t' stuff their owd wallets wi' mate,
    Till they're as reaunt an' as brawsen as frogs ;
But for me I'm content, when I've paid deawn my rent,
    Wi' enoogh t' keep me up i'm clogs - ogs.
                          Wi' my pickers, &c.

An' some are too idle to use their own feet,
  An' mun keawer an' stroddle i'th' lone ;
But when I'm wheelt or carried i'tll be to get buried,
  An' then dicky-up wi' owd one - Jone.

                        Wi' my pickers, &c.

Yo' may turn up yo'r noses at me an' th' owd dame,
  An' thrutch us like dogs again' th' wo ;
But as long's I con nayger I'll ne'er be a beggar,
  So I careno' a cuss for yo' o - o.

                        Wi' my pickers, &c.

Then, Margit, turn reaund that owd hum-a-drum
        wheel,
  An' my shuttle shall fly like a brid ;
An' when I no lenger con use hont or finger,
  They'll say while I could do I did - id.

                        Wi' my pickers, &c.

LANCASTRIANS IN LONDON.

YE sons of Gaunt, " time-honoured " sire
   Of Lancashire's proud family,
I send you greetings from our home,
   The home of our great ancestry ;

Our rugged hills, and valleys deep :
   The dearest spot to you and me ;
The brightest star in England's crown ;
   This gem " set in a silver sea."

For deeds of valour we're renowned,
   On field and flood our flag hath waved,
On Cressy's walls, and Agincourt
   The storm of battle we have braved.

But Peace hath her victories as well
   As those of desolating war ;
And conquests on the field of toil,
   Than those of arms the nobler far.

We've shared those victories—nay, led
   The van throughout the bloodless strife,
Now see our villages and towns,
   Are teeming with industrial life.

At wakes, or fair, on village green ;
   At song, or dance ; at work, or sport ;
Our " Lankey " lads, and lasses too,
   Are known to be a " gradley sort."

Let these bear witness to her fame—
  Proud Lancashire! who would not prize
A home so fair? why do thy sons
  To thee still turn with longing eyes?

Who could not love a land like this?
  Is there a man with soul so base?
Who's so enrapt with foreign climes,
  As not to own his native place?

May he who home nor country owns:
  Who scorns the soil that gave him birth;
Oh, let him wander where he lists,
  Nor find a resting place on earth.

No county in the roll of shires
  Can match this county Palatine,
For beauty, sense, and homely wit,
  In which are sons and daughters shine.

Then here's to "auld lang syne" my friends,
  Though scattered over land and sea!
We'll pledge in "Jone o' Bardsley's" style,
  The land we love, "our ain countrie!"

Oh, may our brotherhood endure,
  And flourish until Time's decay;
Then seek at last the "Better Land,"
  The measureless Eternity.

*Glasses upside down.

TWO HOMES.

THE mistletoe, with its berries white,
   Resplendent shone in the dazzling light,
As the Lady Abigail sought her bower,
Away from the glare of that festive hour.
Sir Launcelot stole with a lover's tread
To her side ; and, whispering softly, said—
Between each often repeated kiss—
" Oh, what a beautiful world is this !"

No mistletoe hung in the labourer's cot ;
No revelries brightened the labourer's lot,
And the kisses he took were those from his wife—
The sharer of all the joys of his life.
A shawl he'd brought her, of colours gay,
" It's too fine for me," she was heard to say,
" But Jammie, thou'st have an extra kiss—
Oh, what a beautiful world is this !"

Softly the ravishing music came
And filled the soul with a rapturous flame ;
Sometimes its sound was a trill of joy,
That softened down to a maiden's sigh.
Sir Launcelot felt what he could not speak,
As he pressed the Lady Abigail's cheek.
But the lady, o'ercome with her measure of bliss,
Said, " Oh, what a beautiful world is this ?"

Little Billy he sat on a three-legged stool,
And played a tune he had learnt at school,
It was not a shepherd's pipe he blew,
But the tones were sweet, and the air was new,
It sounds like an angel's song of praise,
Though 'tis but an old cracked flute he plays.
" Tell us, dear Billy, what tune it is."
" Oh, what a beautiful woyld is dis !"

My Lady Abigail joined the dance,
And her rubies flashed like Sir Launcelot's glance ;
But the music grew faint, and lights burnt low,
And the janitor's yawn said " It's time to go."
The sky was streaked with the hues of morn,
When Sir Launcelot's henchman sounded his horn ;
And was that the end of all earthly bliss ?
Oh, what a *changeable* world is this !

The baby danced on its mother's knee,
And " crowed " to the music with childish glee.
But the father was silent, his heart was full,
Whilst the revellers' pleasures were waxing dull.
" This life is what we make it," said he,
" A sober joy, or a drunken spree.
" Ours is the happier lot, I wis—
"Oh, what a beautiful world is this !"

MASONIC EPITHO-THRENODY;

AN ALLEGORY.

To His ROYAL HIGHNESS ALBERT EDWARD, PRINCE OF WALES, K.G.,

RIGHT WORSHIPFUL GRAND MASTER OF FREE-MASONS IN ENGLAND;

IN PROSPECT OF THE MARRIAGE OF HIS SON, THE DUKE OF CLARENCE AND AVONDALE, WITH PRINCESS VICTORIA MARY OF TECK, FEBRUARY 27TH, 1892.

THIS day thou add'st another corner-stone,
   To strengthen the foundations of that throne
Which stands embedded in a people's love,
The Architect who plans and rules above ;
And, like a Great Geometrician, draws
His lines, and curves, true to Masonic laws,
Be't thine to measure from in all the things
Thou undertakest ; be't the rule of kings;

Or changing sceptre for a mall, and throne
For the *exalted* chair of Solomon,
Be just, and fear not !

　　　　　　Ere yet be raised
The Master's pedestal, let Him be praised
Whom all the searchers after *light* adore !

　　Now let the cannon boom from every shore !
From the three points of heav'n, *West*, *North*, and
　　South,
Let honours Masonic pass from mouth to mouth,
Until the *East* re-echoes with the sound—
Behold the column risen from the ground !

　　　　Bind well the structure from the widened base;
Prove it with *plumb* and *square*, both line and face ;
And if 'tis strong, and firm, from blemish free,
And solid as one block of Masonry ;—
Faultless in symmetry ; in ambit rare ;
The pride of all that's lovely, sweet, and fair,—
Then to an admiring world it may be said—
This added stone is *well and truly laid*.

THE THUNDERBOLT!

FALLEN is the pillar, shattered is the base
    That was to have upheld it in its place.
Give we the prostrate stone a cypress wreath,
Clothe we the figure with the robes of death.
'Twas but an hour ago the *sons of light*
Basked in the rays of hope, supremely bright.
Aught that the splendour of a court could grace
Was there reflected in a regal face.
The prince, the heir, the king that was to be—
The crowning apex to a dynesty—
Now lies he at the base, where kings ere now
Have lain.   The death-damp on his youthful brow
Tells of a struggle ere he gave his sword
To One whose weapon is His mighty Word.
Stricken to earth, but not by mortal foe—
The lightning came from heaven that laid him low.
The broken column, lying at his feet,
Wrap in the British flag, fit winding sheet;
Cover his breast with flowers wet with tears
Distilled from grief—the grief a nation bears.

Ere yet we lay him in his hallowed bed,
Chant we a requiem o'er the honoured dead.
　　Oh, thou great Architect that built the earth
And all upon it since creation's birth,
Receive into Thy temple this our son,
And place him in the *East*, the shrine he'd won.
Now close the tomb!　Oh, may his soul shine forth
A star resplendent, both in light and worth!
No longer claim we what to heaven was due;
The debt he paid with the last breath he drew,
And now, from earthly bonds for ever free,
He joins the Lodge of IMMORTALITY.

　　　　　　　BRO. BEN BRIERLEY.

ARTHUR SULLIVAN LODGE, 2156,
　　OLD BOAR'S HEAD,
　　　　WITHY GROVE, MANCHESTER.

In Memoriam Poems.

ANNIE,

Only child of Ben. and Esther Brierley;

Born November 7th, 1856. Died June 13th, 1875.

WE thought she was our own for yet awhile;
　　That we had earned her, by our love, of Heav'n,
To be a life's comfort, not a season's smile,
　　Then tears for ever. " 'Tis to be forgiven,"
We deemed her mortal—not an angel sent
　　From out a mission host, on mercy bent.

We were beguiled by her sweet ways of love--
　　The growth of her affections round two stems—
As if they were of her, and from above,
　　We did not note that from her heart the gems
Of her devotion were bestrewn in show'rs
　　Where'er she went, and gathered like spring flowers

And her last words (coherent)—" I have lived,
　　And have not lived "—were full of earthly tone
And utterance.　They, too, our hearts deceived ;
　　Nor were we mindful till, when left alone,
We heard the flutter of a dove-like wing,
　　And a sweet strain, such as the seraphs sing.

Then knew we she had come in mortal guise,
　　To teach us love, and charity, and grace ;
With sun-gold in her hair, heaven in her eyes,
　　And all that's holy in her preaching face.
The scales had fallen, and our vision then
　　Saw that an angel graced the homes of men.

SAMUEL BAMFORD.

Born February 28th, 1788. Died April 13th, 1872.

THIS day a warrior bowed his plume, and died ;
    This day a noble spirit, purified,
Hath pierced the shadows of terrestial night,
And sought enshrinement in the "halls of light."

His was no stagnant life who gives this day
Back to his God a spirit weaned of clay.
For LIBERTY he donned his mail and casque ;
The GODDESS blessing with a smile his task.

He saw that smile irradiate the world
Ere yet he closed his eyes. Boldly unfurled
He the proud banner when the maid was young
For whom he battled, and whose praise he sung.

Nor fought a braver champion in the field
Where men for freedom bled and died. His shield—
" My HOME—MY RIGHT—MANKIND "—the motto bore,
Which to the last, with sheen undimmed, he wore.

Thick were the blows which rang upon his mail ;
Deadly the thrusts that pierced it ; but the trail
Of vanquished pennon, and the droop of crest,
His valour brooked not. His a nobler rest.

Five times unhorsed, and dashed upon the field ;
Yet called he not for quarter, nor would yield
To foes outnumb'ring. Quick to saddle sprang
He yet again,—again his armour rang.

As falls the storm against the stubborn oak,
So fell upon his breast the battle stroke ;
As stands the rock that heeds not flashing sky,
So stood his soul, man's thunder to defy.

And thus contending in that 'sanguined fray,
A victor now, next moment driv'n to bay,
His arm relinquished not its manly thrust
Till lay the foe in ignominious dust.

Then home came he with chaplets on his brow,
To doff his mail and casque.   The knightly vow,
To free his country from a galling yoke,
Fulfilled with honour, he his weapon broke.

And in the evening of his life he lay
Watching the closing of a glorious day ;
And as the summer's sun sinks in the west,
So sank our hero to his quiet rest.

Peace to thy honoured dust !   No lay of mine,
Old soldier ! e'er can reach a worth like thine !
Sing thine own requiem in that noble song
Thy *life* hath writ.   Such themes to *thee* belong.

April 13*th*, 1872.

CHARLES SWAIN,

BORN JAN. 4th, 1803,   DIED SEPT. 22nd, 1874.

ANOTHER vacant chair ! another guest
   Hath left my threshold with his last
      " Good night ! "
'Twas but an hour ago, ere yet the west
   Had lost the amber of its fading light,
One other friend departed, and he said—
"Good bye ! " then sought his everlasting bed.

And gone before were others of the throng
   Who round my board at noon were full of thought
And feeling that found utterance in song,
   Th' eternal watchman's call the ear had caught ;
And Autumn leaves around their footsteps fell
As they, in tones that linger, sang " Farewell ! "

And there are others glancing towards the door,
   As though they saw a shadow on the stair,
With finger pointing to heaven's glittering floor,
   And beck'ning to a festal gathering there.
These shall arise ere yet the night be gone,
And *one*—but which of us ?—be left alone.

He who last left the scene where none can stay,
   Woke with his touch the bosom's tenderest chord,
And sang with fervid lips that noblest lay—
   The love of man and glory of the Lord.
He " breathed of beauty and eternal youth ; "
The " mind," its " grace, divinity, and truth."

And as he moved his fingers o'er the lyre,
   His eyes were ever streaming with a light
Caught from the glow of some celestial fire,
   Shining on worlds beyond the reach of night.
And grew the melody most sweet and clear,
When felt the hand the final touch was near.

As sings the nightingale when all is hushed,
   His song was never heard at noontide hour
Among the crowd of warblers ; but when blushed
   The Night at Day's soft wooing, he his bower
Would seek, and from some solitary spray
Awake the echoes with his roundelay.

But never more shall voice of his be heard
   At our sublunar festivals, nor thought
Flash from his soul in glance as well as word.
   A spell upon his soul the angels wrought ;
And whispering 'neath their pinions, " Brother, come,"
They bore the minstrel to his heav'nly home.

Say not you miss him from his chair to-night,
   Ye who have but another hour to stay,
But watch the flick'ring of the taper's light—
   A symbol of the close of life's brief day—

And be ye ready, brethren, one and all,
That none may hurry at the Watchman's call.

Say—" Peace to the departed ! "   He, ere now,
  Hath heard the songs we list for in our dreams,
But only faintly hear.   Around his brow
  The lustre of immortal glory beams,
In which the smiles of kindred spirits shine,
The scintillations of a light divine.

Oh, why this emptiness of human boasts—
  These songs in praise of perishable wine ?
Our friend the guest is of the Host of Hosts,
  And sips the juice of an eternal vine.
The picture change.   The mourners are the dead
Who wait our coming.   Which of us shall lead ?

JOHN BRIGHT.

DIED MARCH 27TH, 1889.

VANQUISHED at last! and by the only foe
He e'er struck colours to, or yielded spur ;
Leader of hosts to battle, his last blow
  Rang on the mail of the Great Conqueror.
And now his sword lies shattered at his feet—
The chief whose soldiers never knew retreat.

He was no man of peace where might was right ;
  But foremost in the field when war's stern note
Sounded the charge. Then where th' ensanguined
    fight
  Was thickest, he his sabre drew, and smote.
Nor faltered he amidst the glittering storm —
    His war cry—" Peace, Retrenchment, and
    Reform."

He was the Cæsar of the gallant host
  That fought for freedom from the laws which
    bound
The fruits of earth, the Tribune that could boast
  He'd measured blades with nobles, who ne'er found
A blot upon his shield, nor craven fear
Within his breast when, fighting, spear met spear.

But when he saw the enemy retreat,
  And Peace and Plenty spring up at his word,
He doffed his helm, and cast it at his feet,
  And sheathed, unblemished, his victorious sword.
Now twine the bays around the victor's head,
And crown him Prince of our illustrious dead.

J

EDWIN WAUGH.

BORN JANUARY 29th, 1817; DIED APRIL 30th, 1890.

THOU'ST left our choir at last,—the sweetest singer
    That ever warbled o'er thy native heath !
Thy sky-notes, wild, have often made me linger,
    To catch the fulness of their silv'ry breath.

Though caged within the town, thy soul was ever
    Hovering fondly o'er its moorland nest ;
And nought of city life thy heart could sever
    From that dear land where thou hadst hoped to rest.

We're silent now, since thou hast left, and gone
    To join the crowd of songsters gone before ;
Prince, Bamford, Swain have winged it, one by one,
    And songs of homely life are heard no more.

Farewell, old " layrock " ! freed from earthly toil,
    And anguish bravely borne, as 'twere thy cross;
Flutt'ring with broken wing o'er fields of moil,
    To find thy glory in thy country's loss.

Gone are the echoes from the woods and bowers
  Thou'rt won't to visit when the twilight fell,
To mingle wito their melodies and flowers
  Thy songs, so fragrant of the heathery dell.

We mourn thee now as one snatched from the nest,
  And cast away in Death's remorseless train ;
Still we're consoled to think that it were best
  To die, than linger in unceasing pain.

Thou hadst deserved a better fate than this,
  Whose notes have made the welkin ring with joy ;
If ought there be to spare of heavenly bliss,
  Thou'st earned a meed, and that without alloy.

ALLEN MELLOR,

DIED 20TH NOVEMBER, 1838, AGED 54 YEARS.

FELLED, like an oak that hath not known decay,
    But sound in root and branch, as when it grew
In youth's green sapling time—e'er yet the day
    Had come when it had ceased to grow, this true
Giant of the human forest—stricken—fell !
What loss of mind and heart no tongue can tell.

His was a life of vig'rous thought and deed—
    A moral strength with charity combined
To wield a pow'r of help to those in need,
    And nerve anew the weaker of his kind.
In works that make men great he knew no rest
Till he had earned it—now he's with the blest.

Peace be to him whose aim was greatest good ;
    And when the young an aspiration feel
To live a life of usefulness, and would
    Example seek, the finger, true as steel
To magnet, points to him whose death we mourn—
Oh, may we after life reach such a bourne !

AT MY DAUGHTER'S GRAVE.

ON HER NINETEENTH BIRTHDAY.

NOVEMBER'S chills hang in the sullen air,
    The earth is shrouded in funeral gloom ;
The trees around seem fretful, weird, and bare,
    As here I stand beside thy silent tomb,—
My daughter !—loved alike by sire and friend—
Thy Mother's idol, thus to thee I bend !

It seems an age since last I saw thy face,
    Smiling to make e'en death a loveliness ;
And as the scalding tears each other chase
    Down cheeks that ever must be flooded thus,
I feel 'twould be the prime reward of prayer,
To see the glory of thine eyes and hair.

Now cold's the hearth that once thy presence warmed ;
    Dark is the room of which thou wert the light ;
Silent the music which my soul hath charmed,
    When home, and wounded, from the world's stern
        fight.
Thy stool--thy chair--the couch--all vacant now—
Cry through the darkness—" Annie, where art thou ?"

Thy mother nightly lingers at the gate,
   To watch thy coming; and as pale the lights,
She says—" How long—how very long—to wait!
   Such girls as she should not stay out at nights.
All her companions are in bed ere this,
And I'm still waiting for her 'good night' kiss."

This day thou would'st have marked thy nineteenth
        year;
   A day looked forward too long months ago;
That should have brought to us, nor sigh, nor tear,
   But such sweet joy as only parents know.
Who could have dreamt, or felt the galling fear,
That thou would'st hold thy birthday revels here?

A bridal wreath bedecks thy marble brow;
   The robes* enwrap thy form that should have swept
The path which leads to where we plight the vow
   Of love eternal—broken oft, or kept.
If shades commingle 'round thy hallowed bed,
Then thou'lt beseem the bridals of the dead.

Ah, frenzied dreams—ah, visions wild and strange,
   That haunt for aye this wilderness of air!
If in the great, inevitable change,
   Thou, God, seeth fit to show Thy mercies where
Love's blossoms are by thousands largely shared,
This garden of *one* flow'r Thou might'st have spared.

---

*She was buried in full brides-maid's costume, intended to have been worn at the wedding of a cousin. The poor girl begged of her mother, a few days before she died, that she might be allowed to wear the dress on the wedding-day, if not able to attend the ceremony. The request was complied with; it served for her shroud.

They who would tell me life is but a span
　Know not affliction—not the loss of *thee*.
'Tis woe, laid heavy on the soul of man,
　That makes of time a drear eternity.
Life's sunniest moments fly the swallow's flight,
But oh, how slowly creeps the hours of night !

Great God ! whose Will it was to take away
　The *only* lamb that nestled in our fold—
If through His tears who wept on Calvary
　The dear one's face we may again behold ;
Oh, let thy messenger of love descend,
To give assurance such shall be the end !

My pray'r is heard, a voice from out the clouds
　Proclaims in trumpet clangour to the dead—
" Arise ye, shake ye off your mortal shrouds,
　And put on Heaven's eternal robes instead !"
I feel the flutter of an angel's wing,
And hear Heaven's choir their sweet Hosannas sing.

The vision's past ; the gloom is thickening round,
　The mists enwrap me with an icy fold.
But here my soul hath its best solace found,
　And turned to summer warmth the wintry cold.
Thus, hoping, dear, thy face again to see,
I weave those *immortelles* of song to thee !

"TIPS."

" THERE'S no tips for me,"
Said owd Billy o' Dan's;
"'Tho' they're passin' my dur
Both i' wagons, an' vans;
There's bacon, an' cheese,
Comin' throng to th' next heause;
But there's nowt on my shelves,
Would keep life in a meause.

There's whiskey i' gallons,
An' barrels o' stout,
An' brandy i' bottles,
But for Billy there's nowt,
Heaw it is I'm left cawt,
Why I cannot just see;
I'm as good as my neighbours,
But there's no tips for me.

There's turkeys an' geese,
Crommed i' hampers, chock full;
One con hardly help thinkin'
That trade isno' dull.

An' pheasants, an' rabbits,
  An' oysters i' shoals;
An' for those that want roastin'
  There's cart loads o' coals.

I con raise nowt wi' feathers,
  Beawt it be an owd hen
That has seen younger days,
  An' has sarved younger men.
An' here I mun shiver,
  Wi' a tear i' my e'e,
For becose I'm a wayver
  There's no tips for me.

" An' here I mun nagur
  Till late of a neet,
Wi' a rag round my yead,
  An' a brick at my feet,*
An' a waiscoat as slack
  As if hanged on a peg;
An' a stockin' that hardly
  Sticks onto my leg.

If th' rich o' their plenty
  'Twould be nowt but fair
If they'd hond me a morsel
  O' what they con spare.
But I've just tumbled to it,
  I plainly con see,
I'm nobody's workman,
  There's no tips for me.

---

* Handloom weavers used to place a hot brick in the treadle-hole in winter to warm their feet by.

K

" But a day's sure to come,
   An' it isno' far off,
When these worn eaut owd breeches
   They'n tell me to doff.
An' the poor shall appear
   I' grand raiment arrayed,
That mortal ne'er fashioned,
   Nor honds never made.

When this body o' flesh
   Shall be *tipped* in a hole,
An' this spiritual body
   That some call a soul,
From its bondage on earth,
   And its trammels set free,
Shall mount up to glory —
   Then *two* tips for me."

Books,

Pamphlets, Etc.,

W. E. CLEGG, Oldham.

A new Map of Oldham, for Hanging in Offices, 5/- net.

Ben Brierley—

In Three Volumes.   10/6 net ; or, Large Paper edition, 21/- net.

"Ab-o'th'-Yate" Sketches and Other Short Stories. By the
late Ben Brierley.   Edited by the late James Dronsfield (Jerry
Lichenmoss) and containing nine very fine Illustrations (executed
by Collotype process), after Fred W. Jackson, which were specially
drawn for this work.   Also a Portrait of the Author.

Having purchased from Mrs. Brierley her interest in the entire stock of
unsold sets of 'Ab-o'th'-Yate' Sketches, the Publisher has reduced the
prices from 12/6 and 31/6 net to 10/6 and 21/- net respectively.

Thomas Brierley—

THE COUNTRIFIED PIECES OF THOMAS BRIERLEY, of Alkrington, Middleton. 208 pages ; Cr. 8vo. Contains " Th' Silk Wayver's Fust Bearing Whoam to Manchester," and seven other prose pieces ; also sixty-three poetical pieces, besides a number of "Epitaphs," " Toasts," etc., principally in the Lancashire Dialect. Price 1/- net, paper covers ; 1/6 net, cloth.

Samuel Laycock's Works—

WARBLINS' FRO' AN OWD SONGSTER, being the Complete Works of Samuel Laycock. Demy 8vo. Illustrated. Cloth Gilt. New and cheaper edition, 5/-.

Wynford Brierley—

THE CHILDREN'S CHRISTMAS: A Drama for Sunday School and other Entertainments. By Wynford Brierley. Music to Songs (six in number) by Robert Jackson. 6d.

The Lancashire Cookery Book, being a collection of Recipes for Cookery Classes, which are well adapted for Home Use. 2d.

M. R. Lahee—

SYBIL WEST, a powerfully written Lancashire Story. By Miss M. R. Lahee. 5/- cloth.

Edwin Waugh—

ORIGINAL SONGS AND POEMS. By the late Edwin Waugh. Second series, illustrated. Large paper edition, 21/-.

Robert Jackson—

SACRED LEAFLETS. Enlarged (hymn tunes). By Robert Jackson. 2/-

J. F. Lees—

BOOK-KEEPING FOR TERMINATING BUILDING SOCIETIES. Illustrated by a year's transactions of "The Trustworthy Building Society," including a Statement of Accounts and a Balance Sheet, and a Short Chapter on Auditing. By John Frederick Lees, Accountant, Oldham. 3/6 net.

W. Booth—

BOOTH'S GUIDE TO THE ISLE OT MAN, in which are given all the best walks of the Island, with distances accurately stated, and an excellent Map of the Island. The Gradients of Roads are also given. It is the best guide extant for Cyclists. Pocket size, strong and flexible. Price 6d.

W. S. Binns—

A TREATISE IN ELEMENTARY AND ADVANCED DESCRIPTIVE GEOMETRY, with a Chapter on Graphic Arithmetic. By W. S. Binns, F.S.Sc. 8vo., cloth, 2/-.

Robert Booth—

THE COTTON BUYERS' AND MILL MANAGERS' ASSISTANT. By Robert Booth. Net 9d., post free 10d.

Clegg's Ready Reckoner for the Cotton Trades. For ascertaining Cost of Cotton, Cardroom and Spinners' Wages &c. 5/- net.

Clegg's Register of Attendance and Fees. Ninth Edition 9d.
Used exclusively in the Oldham Board Schools and also in other
Schools.

A Sample Free per post on receipt of Sevenpence in Stamps.

Clegg's Oldham Annual, published yearly, containing revised Lists
of Pay Days and other Local Matter. Also Free Insurance Coupon
for all the year. A most useful year book, 2d.; post free, 4d.

Clegg's Local Railway Guide. 1d. monthly.

Clegg's Annual Rent Books. For Saturdays or Mondays, 6d. per
dozen.

Clegg's Rent Books without fixed dates. 9d. per dozen.

Spirit Stock Book, for the use of Hotel Proprietors, Clubs, &c., 1/-

Factory Acts. Printed Forms for hanging in Workshops, Certificates,
Registers, and other Books required.

Hire Agreement Forms, Schedules, etc. "To Let," and other
Window Bills.

FAILSWORTH, MY NATIVE VILLAGE. By Ben Brierley. With
Portrait of the Author and full page illustration of "The Peterloo
Veterans," 2d.

Lancashire Sketches by Ben Brierley—

FRO' WAUGH I' HEAVEN. Poem by BEN BRIERLEY. 1d.

SKITS FRO' WALMSLEY FOWT (No. 1), containing "Th' Boggart o'th' Stump, or The Adventures of a Stuffed Monkey"; "Ab o'th'-Yate's Dictionary"; "Th' Owd Chicken's Main Brew," etc. 1d.

AB-O'TH'-YATE'S LANCASHIRE RECITER. 1d.

AB-O'TH'-YATE AND THE OPENING OF THE MANCHESTER SHIP CANAL. 1d.

HEAW TO DO BEAWT COAL.

LANCASHIRE WIT AND HUMOUR. Price 2d.

SWAPPIN' A MON'S CLOOAS FOR A WOMAN'S. A Blackpool incident. 1d.

SAILIN' FOR BACON and A COLLIER'S SPREE.

The following popular Prose and Poetical Pieces by SAMUEL LAYCOCK have been issued separately. Price 1d. each.

Prose Pieces, sixteen pages, illustrated. 1d. each.

HEAW BILLY ARMATAGE MANAGED TO GET A NEET'S LODGIN'S.

A WHOLESALE KESSUNIN' DOOMENT AT TORRINGTON.

LANCASHIRE KESMUS SINGIN' FIFTY YEAR SIN'.

Poetical Pieces, 1d. each.

BOWTON'S YARD	ODE TO TH' SUN.
WELCOME, BONNY BRID.	TH' PEERS AN' TH' PEOPLE.

Also uniform with the above—

THE ORIGINAL JONE O' GRINFILT, written by Joseph Lees, in 1805.

PICTURES (Black and White) by Local Artists.

Printed direct from the Original Drawings. 6d. each, or in
Suitable Frames, 3/6 per pair.

By Tom Heywood—

" Pug Dog," " Cat," " English Terrier," " Spaniel," " Horse," " Donkey."

By J. H. Hague—

" Limehurst," " Bishop Lake's House at Chadderton Fold."

By the late R. O. Bottomley—

" Chadderton Fold."

The undermentioned Books were not printed by W. E.
Clegg, but, having purchased the entire stock remaining on
the Market, he is disposing of them at greatly reduced prices,
as marked.

Spring Blossoms and Autumn Leaves. A Book of Poems by
the late Ben Brierley. 4/- net, in a new Cloth binding, now offered
at 1/6 net.

Original Songs and Poems. By the late Edwin Waugh. (First
Series). 7/6, offered at 3/6 net.

The Limping Pilgrim. By the late Edwin Waugh. 7/6, offered
at 1/6 net.

The Knobstick. A Story of Love and Labour. By C. Allen Clarke.
2/6, offered at 1/6 net.

www.ingramcontent.com/pod-product-compliance
Lightning Source LLC
Chambersburg PA
CBHW020228030726

47497CB00009B/3004